NYTE PROWLER

NYTE PATROL, BOOK 3

ALEX P. BERG

Cover Art by: Ravven (www.ravven.com)

If you'd like to be notified when more Nyte Patrol novels are released, please sign up for the author's mailing list at: www.alexpberg.com/mailing-list/.

A THREE-RING BINDER SPRAWLED ACROSS MY DESK, ITS open halves stretching from elbow to elbow. Columns of numbers zagged down the pages, written in a cursive chicken scratch that was as legible as the average doctor's prescription slip. The script swam in my vision, and I had to force myself to look away before my eyes started to water. No point in boring into it further, in any case. For as many secrets as the numbers may have held, the general picture they painted was obvious enough.

I grunted as I tipped one side of the heavy binder towards the other. The halves met with a clap, shooting a gout of age old dust into the air. I coughed and sputtered as I pushed myself back from the desk, waving the musty cloud away from my face.

A cool voice slid in amongst my sputtering. "You doing okay there, Lexie?"

My chair squeaked as I swiveled toward the door. Leaning against the frame with arms crossed, shoulders back, and one foot on the jamb stood Dawn. She was a good four inches taller than me, perhaps a couple finger widths shy of six feet. Glossy raven-colored hair fell to the bottom of her ribs, hiding against the equally dark backdrop of a black tank top. She had the sort of lean, muscular body that most people craved but few had the will to ditch ice cream and bread for. With fair skin, cold grey eyes, and high cheekbones, she radiated an exotic aura that was more amorphous than her Filipino heritage suggested. Then again, between Spanish colonization in the sixteenth century, American governance following the Spanish-American war, and Japanese rule during World War II, the Philippines had its fair share of genetic diversity. America wasn't the world's only melting pot.

I coughed once more to clear the fine coating of particles that had deposited upon the back of my throat. "Larry's dust collection is trying to kill me. I'll survive, though—which is more than I can say for our business."

Dawn peeled herself from the jamb and slunk to the stool next to my desk. She moved fluidly but with an unmistakable coiled energy in her muscles, like a panther ready to strike. She lifted a thin, arched eyebrow as she sat. "I hope you're exaggerating."

A car honked outside on West 21st, and someone shouted from the direction of the rundown co-op across the street. It sounded like the same guy who sang along to Jamaican dancehall music at two in the morning.

I sighed. "I think I am, but honestly, I'm not sure. Until you asked me to take a look at our finances, I never realized what I was getting into. Larry must've tracked every expense and revenue stream since the inception of this business. On one hand, it's nice he has records at all. He's always struck me as the kind of guy who wings everything, bills and invoices included. Still, parsing this stuff would be a lot easier if he'd used Quickbooks or Excel instead of eighty-thousand sheets of graphing paper. Seriously, this binder weighs like forty pounds."

Dawn snorted. "You know why he didn't keep track of it on a computer."

I rolled my eyes. "Because it would've blown up the instant he touched it, I know. I still think that's bull crap, for the record. For everything he's taught me about the mystical and arcane arts, he's never been able to explain why magic, which he claims operates along a different dimension than space and time, should have any interference with electronics. I think he just doesn't want to enter the twenty-first century."

Dawn tapped the binder. "Give it to me straight, though. How bad is it?"

"Pretty bad," I said. "For starters, I never realized when you guys lost your previous driver, you ended up having to pay him a severance package."

Dawn shrugged. "Larry destroyed his car. Not a company car. *His* car. He threatened to sue. We had to come to a financial arrangement."

"I suppose that makes sense," I said. "What doesn't is that the Nyte Patrol has outstanding debts to at least a half dozen associates and independent contractors. Did you guys hire outside help before I came along?"

"Every now and then," said Dawn. "Larry would occasionally reach out to other magic users depending on the jobs he had. Honestly, before you joined us, I didn't pay a ton of attention to the day to day operations around here. How much do we owe them?"

"A few thousand here, a few thousand there. It adds up, but those debts aren't the most concerning part. Did you know the Nyte Patrol owns this home? Nyte Patrol LLC, which is the limited liability corporation Larry established, owns this house. Well, technically it's bank owned, but the mortgage is in the LLC's name."

Dawn raised another eyebrow. "I *do* know that. Having the Nyte Patrol own the house was a more equitable proposition than having myself, Larry, or Tank take a personal loan for it. For one thing, we use it as our place of business, so we can write the mortgage off more easily. For another, I don't think a bank would've approved any of us for a mortgage individually when we bought this place."

"That's all well and good except for the fact that the whole point of an LLC is to separate your personal and professional assets from liability," I said. "We're months behind on mortgage payments. If the Nyte Patrol goes under, we lose the house!"

"Well, technically, there are any of number of reasons to organize a business as an LLC. Choice of tax regime. The amount of paperwork involved..."

"*Dawn!*"

Dawn sagged in her seat. "Okay, I hear you. Have you talked to Larry about any of this?"

Now it was my turn to shrug. "I mean... I've tried. You know how he's gotten. Ever since Bill bit him and brought him back from the dead he's wanted nothing to do with any of us. He just stays in the basement doing God knows what." I sighed. "I don't get it. He said he wished he had more time. He made it sound like if there was a way back, he'd take it."

Dawn reached out and touched me on the arm. She cast me a sympathetic glance. "You've got to give him time. It's a difficult transition. He'll come around."

I glanced out the window. The idiot from the co-op was in the patch of dirt outside his apartment, smoking a cigarette with no shirt on. It would only be a matter of time before the dance-hall music started thumping. At least it was only ten in the morning. "Tank hasn't come around."

Dawn rested an elbow on my desk. "That's a whole 'nother mess. He lost his wife. What do you expect?"

"His *ex*-wife," I corrected. "And I understand he might've still loved her, but that doesn't excuse his behavior. He's been more of a recluse than Larry these past two weeks."

"Everyone grieves in their own way," said Dawn. "Trust me. I know Tank better than anyone. He'll work through it."

"But how long is it going to take? Because if my math is right, we don't have the longest of leashes to afford the men in this enterprise." I nudged the accounting binder for emphasis.

Dawn chewed on her lip. Her gaze drifted out the window, and her eyes focused on a point in the distance. As she stared at nothing in particular, I heard a faint rhythmic thumping. The dancehall music. I knew it wouldn't be long...

Dawn slapped my desk. "Screw it. Let the boys wallow. If the Nyte Patrol needs to start earning more money, we're more than up to the task. Let's get to work!"

"How? You think the bank will let us refinance our mortgage?"

"I mean we do some actual *work*, Lexie. Have you not talked to Bill lately? Our phone has been ringing off the hook."

Given Bill was a severed zombie head, he wasn't particu-larly useful outside his bizarre specialty of navigation, but following our defeat of the demon spirit Benedict and his resur-rection of Larry, I'd figured he could be put to better use. I'd bought the guy a Bluetooth headset and upgraded the phone on Larry's desk to one I could pair to the new earbuds. Now Bill worked the landline.

I snorted. "With Larry turning into a hermit, Bill almost never *stops* talking to me. Every time I'm in the living room, he's gabbing my ear off. So yeah, I'm aware of the client list he's amassed. Apparently, killing an ageless demon spirit is the best kind of viral marketing. The issue is the folks who are calling have supernatural problems they want us to solve, and Larry's reluctance to speak to me means I haven't progressed much in my witch training. How am I supposed to exorcise someone's nephew or cleanse a funeral home's chakra without guidance?"

"Not every job that's come our way requires magic, Lexie. Or brawn for that matter. And if what you're telling me about these bank statements is right..." Dawn nodded toward the binder.

I sighed. More than anything, I wanted the Nyte Patrol to work. I'd passed on an internship, eased up on softball practice, strained relationships with family and friends, all because I'd finally found something that excited me, a job I was passionate about. I couldn't let a few outstanding debts destroy my dream before it ever got off the ground.

I stood. "You're right. Let's talk to Bill."

2

I PUNCHED THE DOORBELL AND GOT BUSY WAITING. Somewhere in the parking lot behind me, a middle-aged hipster tinkering with his mid-90's Honda Civic finally convinced it to turn over. A cat mewled from the edge of the concrete railing overlooking the apartments on the second floor above, and some college bros whooped and hollered as they tossed a disc in a misshapen field past the edge of the complex. They were playing ultimate frisbee in the same way that a group of donkeys let onto a tennis court and tossed an orange dodgeball could be said to be playing basketball.

Dawn nudged me as one of the dudes collided into another and the pair collapsed to the yellowed grass. "Graceful, aren't they?"

"That's why our coaches don't let us play intramurals in the off season," I said. "Although I doubt any of the girls on the team would be as dumb or reckless as those guys."

A latch clacked, and I turned in time to see the door open. A young man with a three day old beard and a stained Pearl Jam T-shirt stood in the entrance to his darkened apartment, blinking as he focused his bloodshot eyes on us. "Yeah? What do you want?"

Dawn nodded. "I'm Dawn Blayde, this is Lexie Rodriguez. We're with the Nyte Patrol."

The young man blinked again, and his brow wrinkled in confusion. *"Night patrol?"*

"You're Chaz Peters, right?" The guy sure looked like a Chaz, and if the herbaceous aroma wafting through the open door was what I thought, then he smelled like a Chaz, too. "You called us. Spoke to our secretary, Bill. He said you're dealing with a demon problem?"

"Demon...?" Chaz's eyes widened. "Oh. Yes. *YES. I am.*" He lowered his voice as he said the last part.

Dawn glanced at me. By her look, I knew we were on the same page. "Then I guess we're in the right place. You mind telling us a little bit more about the problem?"

Chaz spoke in more of a hiss than a whisper. "Not out here where *they* can hear us. Come inside. Quick."

Chaz backed away from the entrance and waved us in. As I stepped inside, a thick gloom engulfed me, and the smoky, sweet scent of marijuana fully infused my nostrils. Heavy drapes hung over the windows in Chaz's living room and kitchen, but not a single bulb had been lit to fight back the shadows. I blinked and wrinkled my nose as both of my senses adjusted to the sudden change. Dawn coughed a single time as Chaz closed the front door and shuffled past us toward his couch. On his way there, he paused at a coffee table almost completely hidden underneath a pile of pizza boxes, half-empty bins of Chinese takeout, and piles of books. One of the ones on top was titled *Marxism: Philosophy and Economics.* Apparently, Chaz was an *intellectual* stoner.

Chaz snagged a blown glass pipe and brought it with him to the couch. He pulled a gleaming stainless steel Zippo from his pocket as he sat, flipped the lid, and struck his thumb across the spark wheel. An orange flame burst to life, which he promptly stuck into the end of his pipe. Trails of thin, grey smoke sprouted from the bowl as he puffed on the mouthpiece. When he eventually pulled the thing from his lips, a cloud of smoke drifted aimlessly from between them.

"Feeling better now?" I stood opposite the coffee table, as did Dawn.

Chaz blinked, as if he'd forgotten we were there. "Oh. Sorry. This whole *you-know-what* business has me rattled, you know? Needed something to take the edge off."

I nodded sagely. "I'm sure you did."

Chaz extended the pipe. "Want a hit?"

Dawn waved him off. "It's easier to banish demons with a clear head."

"Shhhhh!" Chaz hissed and looked over his shoulder despite the fact that his couch was pushed against the wall. "Stop referring to them by name. You'll draw their attention."

"I *didn't* refer to them by name," said Dawn. "I referred to them in general. I'm well aware you shouldn't use a demon's name—"

"Shhhhh!" Chaz waved the pipe, sending smoke wafting across the living room. "Stop using that word!"

Dawn lifted an eyebrow in my direction. I gave her the slightest of waves. "Why don't you tell us what the problem is, Chaz? Feel free to substitute language as necessary for, ah... safety purposes."

Chaz cracked his neck. His foot tapped rapidly against the floor as he took another drag from his pipe, and his hand shook despite the supposedly calming effect of the drug he was smoking. "Right. So it started a couple nights ago. Two? Three? I think it was two. That's when I first heard them. Talking. Scheming, really. I had my headphones on at the time, so I thought it was loud neighbors at first, but when I took my buds out I could still hear them, just as quiet, just as raspy. So now I thought someone was in my apartment, right? And it got me all paranoid. So I hid my weed real fast, and I grabbed a lamp, because I didn't have a better weapon nearby, but the lamp was hot and I burned my hand. And then..."

Chaz stuck a finger in the air, but instead of continuing his story, he jammed the end of his pipe back between his lips and started puffing.

"And then, what?" I asked.

Chaz's hand shook as he blew out another cloud of smoke. "That's when I saw it. The portal. In my bedroom, on the wall. Glowing red, rippling with, like, hellish fire. And they called to me. Those... *things*. The D word. I saw one of them, all big and buff and with skin the color of a really bad sunburn. And he had this huge beard, kind of like... Friedrich Engels. And he stared right at me. He opened his mouth, and black smoke poured out, along with this big booming bass. You know, like in dubstep? And that was it, man. *That was it!*"

"That was what?" I asked.

"I got out of there. Never run so fast in my life, not even when I was at a kegger in ninth grade and the cops showed up. Ran out of my bedroom and slammed the door behind me. Haven't been in there since, which is why I need you guys. I was in the middle of a reply to a Reddit post on whether or not private property is, like, really private. I've been itching to finish it ever since." Chaz flipped open a pizza box and scanned the bottom for a spare slice as he took another toke from his pipe.

I glanced over my shoulder. The apartment appeared to be a one bedroom, with the living room, dining, and kitchen all sharing a communal space. I spotted an open door in the hallway with a glint of white porcelain inside, and next to that, a closed door. "Is that it?"

Chaz nodded as he puffed out another cloud of sweet smoke. "Yeah."

"Nothing's come out over the past two days, I'm guessing."

Chaz gave his head a shake. "Thankfully not."

"Have you heard any of those weird sounds since? The dubstep drops? Or smelled any sulfur?"

Chaz stared into the darkness as he took another puff, but he shook his head no.

I nodded. "Can I ask what you were using at the time, Chaz?"

He glanced up at me. *"Using?"*

"You said you had your, ah... *Mary Jane* with you at the time. I'm wondering if you'd been sampling anything else."

Chaz's brow furrowed. "Well, there were the mushrooms... No, wait. I think I took those on Monday? I might've had some mescaline... Not really sure."

Dawn touched me on the arm. "Lexie? Can I speak to you in private?"

Chaz wasn't even looking at us, his bloodshot eyes half closed as he tried to remember what drugs he'd taken. "Sure."

Dawn drew me to the furthest corner of the kitchen space. Her voice was little more than a whisper, but there was an angry hiss to it. "What do you think you're doing?"

"What does it look like I'm doing?" I said. "I'm trying to

walk Chaz to the obvious conclusion that he's tripping balls and imagined the whole thing."

"Exactly," hissed Dawn. "Bill threw us a softball and you're not even going to swing at it—pardon the metaphor."

I felt a warm sense of irritation creeping up my neck. "What are you proposing? That I lie to this guy? Tell him we'll solve his demon problem only to go into his room, bang around, and pronounce the demonic ghost of Friedrich Engels is defeated?"

"Yes," said Dawn, her voice creeping up in volume. "That's exactly what I expect you to do. Do you not remember our conversation this morning? The outstanding debts? The past due mortgage payments? How eager do you think Chaz is going to be to open his wallet after we break it to him that the demons in his bedroom are a result of one too many bong hits?"

I pressed my fingers against my temple. "Dawn... This isn't what I imagined. Our first stop before lunch we literally helped a lady pull her cat out of a tree. That's a job for firefighters —*volunteer* ones. Now we're going to lie to some cracked out bohemian to make a few bucks? I feel dirty. Where's the action, the adventure, the search for justice?"

Dawn's face softened. "Lexie, I don't want to burst your bubble. Passion is important in any job, but at the same time, this *is* a job. We're guns for hire, sometimes literally. Most of the time we don't get to choose who we work with, and given we're short a few of our crew and our bank account is in the red, we have less leeway than normal in picking and choosing clients. So we do the job, cash the paycheck, and move on to the next one."

I sighed. "You're right. But I feel slimy lying to this guy, even if we do need the money."

"So don't lie," said Dawn. "Get creative with the truth."

I nodded, and we returned to Chaz. Luckily for us, he

hadn't moved, though his leg was tapping against the floor even faster than before.

I took a deep breath and engaged my creative muscles. "Good news, Chaz. We think we've figured out the root of your demon problem. We're going to head into your room. Check things out. If it's what we think it is, shouldn't take more than five minutes."

"Really?" Chaz took another hit off his pipe. "Gosh, that would be amazing. I haven't slept in my bed in like two days."

Or at all, I thought. "Yeah. Stay here, okay?"

I nodded to Dawn and we crossed to the bedroom. I cracked the door enough for us to sidle in. Like I expected, a glowing portal didn't greet us from the far wall, only the stale scent of marijuana and cigarette smoke. The drawer on Chaz's desk hung open, and inside I spotted a few plastic baggies full of pot. A few more with mysterious powders lay alongside them.

I rolled my eyes and sat in the desk chair. I checked my email on my phone and played a few of those bubble popping games while Dawn did the same. After six or seven minutes, I gave Dawn a nod. "Think that's enough?"

"Probably," she said. "Let's give our customer the good news."

As it turned out, the news did make Chaz happy. But I didn't feel any less skeezy telling him the demons wouldn't bother him anymore than I would've telling him the straight truth.

3

I PARKED MY '94 CHEVY SUBURBAN IN A FREE SPOT AT THE front of the run-down strip mall. The lettering on the window storefront before me read *Nine Moons Witch Supply* in an elaborate, cursive script. Below that in a blocky font more reminiscent of cheap Chinese food joints and massage parlors were the words *Psychic Readings, Healing Crystals, Occult Surplus,* and *We Also Unlock iPhones.*

I glanced at my phone's GPS. "This can't be the right place."

"On the contrary," said Dawn. "This *has* to be the right place." She hopped out of the truck and shut the door behind her with a clang.

I followed her out and into the store. A chime attached to the top of the door rang as I pushed my way through. A scent of patchouli incense hung in the air, and fluorescent tube lights emitted a high-pitched hum from their rectangular troffers. Random tchotchkes packed shelves that stood too close to one another. I spotted displays for tarot cards, scented candles, and magic crystals, the latter of which I was almost entirely sure were colored glass. Dreamcatchers of various sizes dangled from rotating mobiles, and a display in front of me lauded the healing effects of a balm made from marigold, rose, chamomile, and beeswax—just $29.99 for a four ounce container. I guess it was still cheaper than many commercial cosmetics.

Dawn sauntered over to the checkout kiosk, basically a glass case filled with refurbished phones two generations behind the latest models. No one stood there, but a silver bell sat on the counter. A small sign next to it read "Ring for assistance."

Dawn snorted. "What's the point of a door chime if they're not going to listen for it?"

I shrugged, and Dawn tapped the bell. It rang, filling the store with a melodious tinkle. To be fair, it was a lot louder than the chime on the door.

A muffled voice responded from in back. "Just a moment!"

I joined Dawn by the counter. A sign within the glass case detailed the store's policy on repairs and made sure to state in bold letters that any work done on phones voided existing service provider warranties.

"Remind me what we're here for again?" said Dawn.

"Bill said it was a tracking job," I said. "I don't know the details, but he was quick to tell me we couldn't be any worse at it than Larry, so we might as well give it a shot."

"He really has a way with words, doesn't he?" said Dawn.

I heard a rustling, followed by the same mellow voice I'd heard from behind the stacks of pseudo-mystical crap. "Sorry about that. How can I help you?"

I turned to find a woman who looked like the African-American version of Sybill Trelawney, the divinations teacher from the Harry Potter movies, making her way toward us. Frizzy black hair poured from underneath a patterned yellow and black headband, one that matched the simple dress and shawl she wore. Thick-rimmed glasses magnified her bright amber eyes, and about five pounds of necklaces, amulets, and bangles hung from her neck and wrists.

"Hi," I said. "I'm Lexie Rodriguez. This is Dawn Blayde. We're with the Nyte Patrol. Are you Augusta Shade, by chance?"

The woman nodded as she crossed to the edge of the kiosk. "Ah, yes. I was wondering when you'd arrive. The person I spoke to on the phone wouldn't commit to a time and date. I didn't know if *anyone* would come help, to be honest."

"Yeah, that's Bill," said Dawn. "We're working with him on his customer service. He doesn't have a lot of experience."

Augusta smiled. "New hire?"

"No. Internal reassignment, but Bill's never worked the phones before, despite his age. I guess that's what happens when you spend most of the past two hundred years in a glass jar."

Augusta's eyebrow rose, and I nudged my partner. "Uh, Dawn? Maybe ixnay on the specifics about Bill?"

"Oh, you won't alarm me," said Augusta. "What is this Bill friend of yours? A sprite, or perhaps a jinn? Some of the elder races can live half a millennia, or so they'll tell you. Not sure if I believe them. They're tricksy little buggers, for the most part."

Augusta made the claim without any trace of sarcasm, and her raised eyebrow gave her a look of curiosity more than skepticism. "Ah... Bill's a severed zombie head, to be honest. Are you telling me you actually believe in magic and the supernatural? That this witch supply shop isn't for show?"

"For show?" Augusta's second eyebrow joined the first.

"Miss Rodriguez, I assure you I take my business seriously. I sell only the highest quality witch and wizarding supplies."

I glanced at the shelves filled with cheap junk. "Uh..."

Augusta followed my gaze. "Not that stuff. Most of it is imported from Mexico or China. I sell it to folks who only pretend to follow the lifestyle. I keep the real supplies in back. If you follow me, I'll show you. That's where the break-in occurred, anyway."

"Break-in?" asked Dawn.

Augusta paused mid-step. "Yes. I'm guessing Bill didn't explain that to you."

"Not *fully.*" *Or at all,* I thought. "We're going to have to put Bill through some more extensive training."

Augusta shrugged. "It's alright. Easier to show you what happened and explain it in person. It's a strange situation anyway. Hard to give a sense of it over the phone."

Augusta shuffled off towards an Employees Only door, turning sideways to fit through the gap between a pair of tightly stacked shelves. Dawn slipped through the same gap effortlessly. Thankfully, so did I. I may not have had her goddess-like figure, but I least I had flat abs.

The employee door creaked as Augusta opened it. Her hand flicked to a switch on the wall and the lights above flickered to life. She waved her hands at the shelves that packed the back as tightly as the front. "Here's where I keep the *real* inventory."

On first glance, the stuff filling the shelves looked like the same kind of crap Augusta had in front—balms and salves, bundles of herbs, candles, vials, brown paper packets with labels that looked handwritten but were nonetheless printed—but a pause and a closer look at the goods next to me suggested the quality was higher. The crystals might've actually been crystalline as opposed to glass, the candles included ingredients like dittany and sunwort, and the packages of playing cards looked like they'd been sourced from ancient barns combed over by those picker guys on the History channel.

"Over here," said Augusta as she shuffled past another shelf. "Mind the scrying orbs. I've knocked more than one over myself. Really need to reorganize those, if I'm being honest."

I squeezed past the precariously piled translucent orbs, following Dawn through tight aisles. In front of me, Augusta came to a stop and waved her hand. *"This* is where it happened."

I stepped from between the clutches of wire shelves into the middle of an indoor grow operation, but not one filled with distinctive notched leaves that might be dried and sold to Chaz for recreational use. Rather, it was as if I'd walked into the outdoor portion of one of those home and garden stores. Racks with five shelves apiece were filled with small flowering plants and herbs, with full spectrum lights and misters hanging over them.

Augusta had stopped in front of one particular rack that seemed to have been hit by a tornado. Not a single potted plant on the thing remained upright. Most of them had been knocked to the ground, where their soil had spilled across the polished concrete. Bits of leaves and stems littered the ground alongside the dark earth.

Augusta wiggled a finger at the mess. "I would've cleaned it up, but I figured you'd need to investigate. I've watched enough crime shows to know not to do that."

I nodded, trying to act like I knew what I was doing. "Right. So, ah... what happened first? That led to this, I mean?"

Augusta frowned. Her foot tapped the floor as she looked at

us carefully. "Bill didn't tell you anything *at all* about why I called, did he?"

Dawn shrugged apologetically. "Sorry. We've been down a couple of our more senior patrol members for the past two weeks. We're still trying to work out the kinks, but we'll do whatever we can to help. You just have to fill us in on the details."

Augusta took the admission more coolly than most would've. "It's alright. I know how hard it is to find good help. Regardless, this is what I meant when I said we had a break-in. I found the display like this two days ago when I opened the store in the morning. The entire crop of masterwort, lustwort, and hogweed—completely ruined! And that's not all. Whoever got in tracked dirt all around back here. I'm also pretty sure they rearranged my collection of animal hair tufts, and on top of that, they took half of the graduation robes off their hangers."

"Graduation robes?" I said.

"For those attending wizarding school," said Augusta. "I told you, I stock *all* witch and wizarding supplies."

"Have you called the police about this?" asked Dawn.

Augusta snorted. "Please. For one thing, I don't have any interest in revealing to the authorities my collection of shrunken heads and voodoo supplies, but more importantly, they're not going to take me seriously. The mundies never do. That's why I called you. People I can trust. People who can actually help me track who broke into my store and manhandled my wares."

A shiver of excitement ran through me. In the months I'd spent as part of the Nyte Patrol, I'd only been presented with one or two real mysteries. More often than not we'd been relegated to performing demeaning fetch quests and telling half-truths to baked out morons like Chaz. Of course, with the shiver of excitement came an equal shiver of concern, because despite spending the odd hour or two with Frank Connors, head of Austin's police special investigations unit, I really didn't know the first thing about being a detective.

I took a breath to still my nerves. "So, to be clear then, Ms. Shade—whoever broke in ruined your plants, reorganized your animal fur collection, and tried on some of your robes, but they didn't steal anything?"

"Well, I'm not sure if that's true," she said. "Given the mess they made of my worts and weeds, I can't say with total certainty if they harvested them, ate them, or shredded them out of spite. But as far as the rest of the inventory, you're correct. As far as I can tell nothing was taken. It's one of the many confusing elements of this assault on my business."

"Are there more?"

"Sure," said Augusta. "How about the fact that whoever broke in locked up after themselves when they left?"

Dawn's brow furrowed. "Come again?"

"Two mornings ago when I found this, the whole store was locked up as usual," said Augusta. "Front door was locked. The back door was locked. The Employees Only door was locked. None of my windows were broken. No signs of forced entry anywhere. Unless someone teleported in here, they must've locked up behind them, and before you ask, I *did* consider teleportation as an option. I didn't find any traces of magical circles, however. Perhaps you can detect some where I couldn't."

"Maybe it wasn't a break-in," I said. "Do you have other employees?"

Augusta shook her head sternly. "Only two, and I've spoken to both of them. They've been with me a long time. I trust them implicitly. Not only did they assure me they had nothing to do with this, but both of them could account for their keys the night of the break-in."

"Maybe someone copied one of the keys," I said. "Just because they had eyes on them two nights ago doesn't mean that's always been the case."

"Reel it in, Lexie," said Dawn. "No one would go to that level of effort to break into a magical supply shop and then not steal anything—no offense, Ms. Shade."

Augusta seemed to take a little, regardless of Dawn's preemptive apology. "Well, someone made a mess of my store. My plants didn't shred themselves."

"Of course not," said Dawn. "But that doesn't necessarily mean some*one* is at fault. I don't know much about masterwort and lustwort, but hogweed is a drug. It affects sprites, brownies, and a few other things, right?"

Augusta nodded reluctantly. "Fae catnip is what some call it. Its reputation is well deserved, but I already know what you're thinking. Wild sprites didn't do this. They can't get through locked doors any easier than men and women can."

"Could've been a raccoon," I said. "They like to break into air conditioned spaces on hot summer days. Have you checked to see if there are holes on your roof or exterior walls?"

Apparently, suggesting Augusta's problems were caused by trash pandas was a bridge too far. Her eyebrows lifted slowly and her nose turned noticeably upward. "I don't have a *raccoon problem,* but if I did, are you suggesting you wouldn't be able to help me with it? I need *someone* to track down the intruder who violated my rights and privacy, human, animal, spirit, mineral, or otherwise. Is that something you can do, or should I call a pest exterminator instead?"

I glanced at Dawn. She tilted her head toward me almost

imperceptibly, but she rubbed her thumb and forefingers together in the universally accepted gesture for cash—something we still desperately needed.

"No worries, Ms. Shade," I said. "Whoever broke into your store, you can rest assured we're going to catch them." *Even if it means busting out the possum traps,* I thought. *Oh, the things I do for my job.*

4

The chime sounded as we pushed back into the parking lot. Dawn groaned as the shop door banged shut behind us.

"Don't give me that," I said. "You think I knew what we were getting into? Bill told me it was a tracking mission. If I'd known we'd be getting roped into trapping vermin..."

Dawn held up a hand. "My frustration right now is with Bill. *Tracking, my ass...*"

"We could go back in there. Tell Augusta the job isn't right for us."

Dawn shook her head. "No. For one thing, it's unprofessional. Once you accept a job, you see it through. And even past the whole money issue, you have to admit the details of the break-in that Augusta laid out are..." Her face twisted up.

"Intriguing?"

Dawn smirked. "I was going to use a spicier adjective, but yeah. I still think the most likely scenario is that an armadillo crawled into the back of her shop and helped itself to an all you can eat buffet of mind-altering herbs, but if not... I don't know. There could be something going on."

"I sure hope so," I said. "The case has so much promise."

Dawn peered at me skeptically. "Still hoping to find action and adventure, are you? I thought you would've learned by now how hazardous to your health those things can be."

"Hey. I've done as you suggested. We've taken every job with a paying customer, regardless of their problem. If we get roped into some insane trek into the underworld or versus a world-eating elder god, it's on you."

Dawn snorted. "I suppose it is."

I paused outside my car door. "So assuming we're *not* dealing with a rodent problem, what do you think our first step should be?"

Dawn looked at me across the hood of my truck. "Normally when we've tackled jobs like this one, I'm the one who argues for rational approaches while Larry tries to convince the rest of us that some obscure spell would shed light on the situation. Sadly, Nine Moons doesn't have a security system, so that limits our options. Still, we could start by looking around the outside for points of entry and talking to the neighboring businesses, see if they saw anyone suspicious lurking about."

I chewed on my lip at the thought of Larry. "Just out of curiosity, how often would Larry get his way and use the magic based approach?"

"More often than not. And it worked *way* more often than I care to admit. That's the thing about magic—"

The rumble of a V8 engine drowned out the rest of Dawn's sentence as a flat black Cadillac Escalade pulled up alongside my Suburban on the passenger side. It wasn't just the roar of the engine that drew my attention, though. The thing looked like the sort of vehicle the Secret Service would roll around in, with tinted windows, gunmetal rims, and an added heft to it, as if it had been armor plated.

The engine died with a grumble, and Dawn snorted. "Oh, great."

I didn't get a chance to ask what was going on as the driver's side door opened and out popped an enormous, gourd-nosed gump. The guy was roughly six and a half feet tall, with a shaved head and a close-cropped goatee. He wore a black T-shirt and black pants, with black combat boots and a black flak jacket thrown over his chest. A pair of black aviator sunglasses perched from his misshapen eggplant of a nose. He ripped the latter off as he slammed the door shut behind him.

"Well, well, well," he said as he took a step toward Dawn. "If it isn't the Nyte Patrol. I thought you guys were nocturnal."

Dawn's voice frosted the air despite the central Texas summer heat. *"Otis.* What do you want?"

That's when I remembered him. Otis Zachary Pacheco, part owner of the monster hunting conglomerate known as BSI, or Brute Squad Incorporated. I'd met him once during the same underground lava pit melee where I'd encountered Angus O'Neill and Dawn's girlfriend, Charity Peterson. In the full light of day, he was uglier than I remembered him, although perhaps it was a function of him not having his better half beside him to lighten the aesthetic load.

Speak of the devil... The Escalade's passenger side door slammed shut, and none other than Otis's partner—and I think wife?—turned the corner. Jane Fettercross was the Yin to his Yang, maybe five foot two and a hundred and ten pounds soaking wet. Though she also seemed to favor the color black, her wardrobe was the business formal version of Otis's commando garb. Her pants were flared at the bottom with a tight crease along the centerline that held firm as she walked. A crisp white dress shirt with wide cuffs and an even wider collar clung to her slender frame, cinched tight to her by a black corset that was trimmed to look like a suit vest. Her brown hair had been pulled back into a smooth pony tail, and designer sunglasses shaded her eyes.

"Afternoon, Dawn." She cocked her head and pulled her glasses down on her nose as she peered at me. "And you were... *Lily?*"

"Lexie." I stepped around the front of the truck and sidled next to Dawn. "So, what's up with you guys. I haven't seen you since—"

"Since you deliberately ignored our FBI mandate and nearly got us all killed?" Jane pulled the glasses the rest of the way off and sneered at us. I couldn't tell if she looked more like a stock photo of an angry CEO or a naughty businesswoman in a porn movie, minus the cleavage.

"Give me a break," said Dawn. "You guys always try to pull rank on everyone, even people who don't work for you. You're not police and never will be, so whatever the hell you're here for, spit it out and get on your way."

Otis pulled his sunglasses off and tucked them onto his shirt collar. "Relax, Nyte Patroler. We're not here to throw down. We were called to investigate a break-in."

I glanced at the storefront. "At Nine Moons?"

Jane snorted. "No. At the Taco Shack up the street. We needed to get our steps in."

A smoldering heat crept up my neck, and my hand clenched into a fist. Admittedly, I'd only ever spent a minute or two in Jane's presence and that had been bookended by adrenaline-fueled battles against demonic hell beasts, but I didn't remember her being such a bitch.

Dawn crossed her arms, and her jaw tightened. "Might as well pack up and go home. We're tackling the Nine Moons case."

Jane took a half step forward, but Otis kept her from moving any further with a hand to the corset. "I don't think so, Dawn. The owner called us this morning and offered us her business. We intend to see the job through. Unlike you guys, we actually care about our professional reputation."

"Augusta called us first, Otis."

"And you must've given her reason to think you'd do a terrible job or not help her at all because she called us afterwards," said Otis. "Come on, Dawn. You know how this works. You get paid for results, not for staking claims. Given the extra offers you've been getting since that business with the O'Neills, did you really think we wouldn't cross paths at some point?"

Dawn's nostrils flared. "How do you guys know about that?"

"Didn't you know?" said Jane, her voice icy. "You're the talk of the supernatural community. Everyone wants a piece of you. It's part of our job to notice that sort of thing."

Dawn glanced at me before returning her gaze to Penn and Teller. "Is that what this is about? You guys are *intimidated* by us? You think we're going to steal your business?"

Jane smiled as she drew her sunglasses back over her eyes. "That's not much of a concern at this point, but they do say the best defense is a good offense. Best of luck with the rest of your job offers. Hopefully a few of them are still around when you get to them."

I blinked, trying to process what was going on. "Are you guys for real?"

Jane turned toward Nine Moons without another word, but Otis hung back. Like his partner, he smiled as he pulled his glasses from his shirt and slipped them back on. "You ladies have a nice night. Oh, and give my regards to Larry. A little birdie told me he's feeling under the weather. I'd hate for that to affect your business."

He turned and followed Jane, disappearing into Nine Moons to the tinkle of the door chime.

I turned to Dawn, the heat having spread from my neck to my cheeks. "What the hell was that about? Are they seriously trying to muscle us out? And how the hell do they know more about our business than we do?"

Dawn's teeth squeaked as she ground them together. "High profile cases put a target on your back, but I never saw this coming. *Damnit.* The last thing we need is to get into a turf war with BSI. They've got more manpower than we do, more capital, more everything. If they decide to tighten the screws, say hello to bankruptcy. And for Otis and Jane to be here in person? Son of a..."

The anger within me started to fade, replaced instead with creeping dread. "So what you're saying is, we need backup?"

Dawn nodded once. "We definitely need backup."

5

I KNOCKED ON THE DOOR TO THE BASEMENT FOR THE second time. "Larry? Are you in there? Can I come in?"

I leaned in close to see if I could hear anything. There were definitely sounds coming from downstairs. The occasional thump, bump, and what I thought was a curse, which gave me confidence it wasn't some beast that had eaten Larry during a summoning gone wrong. At least, it gave me *some* confidence.

I waited a few seconds. When I still didn't get an answer, I tested the handle. It twisted, and when I pushed, the door swung open. I'd half expected Larry to have installed a padlock on the thing when none of us were paying attention.

The light in the stairwell wasn't on, but a pale orange glimmer nonetheless shone from deep within the subterranean gloom. "Larry?"

The stairs creaked, letting loose decades old groans as they bent under my feet. When I'd first moved in with the rest of the Nyte Patrol, I hadn't realized the home had a basement. Few central Texas homes did, given that you had to dig into solid limestone at about five feet down. That was exactly what someone had done here, but it hadn't been anyone who'd been born during the last half century. Rock walls brushed against my arms as I descended the steps, untouched by paint or clear coat and rough as they would've been the day the mason's chisel cleaved them from their hardened siblings. The beams holding the house above were weathered—age-darkened posts that could've been salvaged from a barn, dulled by oils and moisture.

The air cooled noticeably as I dipped below the surface of the earth, but my nose wrinkled at the smell. The lower temperatures should've slowed the decay of whatever was going bad down there, but it nonetheless smelled like someone had left a sack of garbage in the sun for a couple days. Of course, given how little I'd seen of Larry the last two weeks, the garbage might've been accumulating a lot longer than two days. At least I didn't hear the buzzing of any flies.

I made a ninety degree turn as I reached the bottom of the steps, hopping onto a floor of packed earth. A hard base of stone existed somewhere beneath my feet, but decades of dust and microbial decay had hidden the limestone under a thin veneer of organic matter. The orange light I'd seen earlier played along the exposed beams and poorly shielded electrical cables above me, but I couldn't spot the source of the glow thanks to all the crap in the way. Cardboard boxes had been piled high on both sides of the stairs, creating a narrow path further into the basement, but they were far from the only contributors to the hedge maze of junk that loomed before me. I skirted around an antique bookcase filled with yellowed romance paperbacks, ducked underneath an overturned kayak, and stepped over a metal rack packed with canning jars as I ventured deeper into the space.

"Larry? It's me, Lexie. Where are you? We need to talk."

A voice responded, muffled by walls of cardboard and porcelain dolls swaddled in bubble wrap. "Go away."

My heart jumped at the sound of his voice. I'd missed talking to him, if I was being honest. "Come on, Larry. Don't be like that. You can't hide in the basement forever."

I heard a snort. Was it to my right? It was hard to tell. "Try me."

I flattened my body as I squeezed between a stack of boxes and a pile of yellow leather suitcases that had Pan American luggage tags hanging from them. When did that airline go out of business? The seventies? "Bill misses you. We all do. We just want to talk."

Larry's voice fluttered over, now sounding as if it had come from my left. "I'm not being subtle. Leave me alone. I have things to do."

The crack I'd snuck through spat me into a clearing of sorts. Floor rugs, plastic bins, and a broken washing machine had been pushed to the side, opening up a patch of free dirt roughly six feet by six. Larry had drawn a circle in the dust with a hexagon in it. Flecks glimmered from the lines in the dirt, something with a metallic glimmer. Either Larry had added steel shavings from a support beam to his circle, or he'd stumbled across the basement's stash of arts and craft supplies.

"That's why I'm down here," I said. "We all have things to do, and when I say we, I mean the collective we. You, me, Dawn, Bill, Tank. The Nyte Patrol. You realize it's been two weeks since we defeated Benedict, right?"

I spotted a flicker of motion between boxes. "I haven't lost track of time, Lexie. In fact, I'm more keenly aware of it with every passing day."

"What's that supposed to mean?"

Larry's voice grew tense. "It means *I* have work to do. Me. By myself. Without you involved. You're supposed to be running this business now. If you have problems, deal with them yourself."

I tried to follow the motion but got blocked by an antique dresser that looked like it weighed about a ton. I'd have to head back to the crack by the luggage. "While I appreciate your faith in me, things aren't that simple. You'd know that if you weren't hiding down here night and day. Our phones have been ringing off the hook since we banished Benedict from our plane of existence. While that's generally a good thing—lord knows we need the income—it means we have a lot of customers and not enough people to handle their problems."

"So hire someone," said Larry. "That's what I did with you."

"God damnit, Larry. I'm not hiring someone else when I have a perfectly good wizard hiding in the basement. And yes, a wizard's input specifically would be quite helpful. Bill's been collecting our clients' names and sorting their cases. A lot of them require magical expertise. He's handed some of the more mundane stuff to Dawn and me, but there are a lot of jobs we could be working right now that I've had to delay because the wizard who's supposed to be working for us has turned into a groundhog in winter. So get your shit together and come help me."

I heard an exasperated sigh as I popped back into the main box-lined path, coming from the direction of a box spring wrapped in pale blue plastic. "I do not know how to be more clear. I'm too busy to help you at the moment. And you know what? To be perfectly honest, I don't *want* to help you right now."

The statement hit me in the gut with the strength of a

boxer's jab. It stopped me in my tracks, but I couldn't totally blame Larry for his anger.

I took a deep breath and let it out slowly. "Okay. I deserved that, but at least I know where it's coming from. I've said it before, but I'm willing to say it again. *I'm sorry.* I'm sorry I brought you back from the dead. I thought I was doing you a service. When we were standing there in the spirit world, both of us mourning your passing, you told me you wished you had more time. That you wished you didn't have to say goodbye. What was I supposed to think?"

Larry's voice was a little deeper than usual and had a tautness to it, like a violin string that had been strung too tight. "I told you I was okay with it. I told you to move on."

"Well then you gave me conflicting information. It's as much your fault as mine." I grimaced as I ducked underneath the box spring, which sagged as it leaned against a wire rack packed tight with more boxes. I shouldn't have snapped, but why couldn't Larry accept my apology, damnit?

I pushed forward into another small cleared space. The mattress that accompanied the box spring had been freed from its plastic cage and dumped on the ground next to the wall. An overflowing waste bin had been parked next to it, and the source of the orange glow that filled the basement flickered behind it, waving through the translucent white plastic of the bin. Larry sat opposite the bed in an office chair, mostly hidden in shadow. He had his back to me, his hat pushed low over his head and the hem of his leather duster brushing the floor.

I stood there for a moment, the stench from the wastebasket making me frown. Was he throwing food scraps away in there? "Well? Aren't you going to face me?"

Larry shook his head. *"It's as much my fault as yours.* I'd love to hear you explain to me how *THIS* is *MY FAULT!"*

Larry surged out of his chair, spinning to face me. I took a step back, but what I saw made me freeze. Larry's ragged beard hadn't been trimmed in the two weeks he'd been in the basement, but behind it, his skin had turned a pale grey with sickly green and yellow splotches around his eyes. Open sores dotted his lips, and his dark, greasy hair stuck to the sides of his face from a mixture of dried sweat and accumulated body oils. More than anything, though, it was his smell that shocked me. It wasn't the garbage that was going south. It was *him.*

"Oh my God. Larry, I'm..."

"Sorry?" he spat. "Guess what? Sorry doesn't change *this!* Honestly, did you ever stop to think what would happen when you had Bill bite me? Did it occur to you what the consequences of bringing me back as a zombie might be? Of what might happen physically? *Of course not!* You never considered that my flesh would rot and fall off my bones. That I'd never be able to find acceptance from literally anyone ever. That I'd never be able to show my face in public again. Otherwise you would've let me die in peace, like I wanted!"

Tears welled in my eyes, not so much from being yelled at but at being confronted with the true nature of what I'd wrought. Larry was right. I'd made the choice. I hadn't thought it through. "I... I thought it was what you wanted. It all happened so fast. I was hurt. I wanted you back."

"Exactly! This is about what *you* wanted, not what *I* wanted! *And you ruined my life!"*

I hung my head, feeling the first of the tears break free and roll down my cheek. I'd made mistakes before. Everyone has.

But this was the first time that I had no idea how to make amends for the choices I'd made.

My chest ached as I forced air into my lungs. "Larry... Maybe there's a way to reverse it. There's got to be some spell, some antidote..."

"Are you dense?" Larry's anger washed over me. "What do you think I've been doing down here for the past two weeks? Reading Kafka's *The Metamorphosis* and pondering on the frailty of existence? Of course I've been trying to find a cure!"

"We could work together," I offered. "If we pooled your magical ability with mine, maybe we could do something."

Larry snorted in derision. "*Your* magical ability? You think that's going to make a lick of difference? You barely know the first thing about magic!"

Which was sort of the point, I thought. I took a deep breath to settle my emotions. "Larry, please. Come up. Together, we can help you. I know we can. And besides that, we need you. I need you, and not just for you to teach me about magic and help lighten the load. We need you to be a part of the team, again."

I lifted my head enough to catch the withering glance Larry cast me. "You want *my* help? After everything I've told you? Get the hell out of my basement. *Now!*"

As someone who was fully aware of my own failings, I was willing to take a certain amount of abuse, but even I had my limits. A frothy rage surged up, filling the aching hole in my chest. "Fine! Be that way! Who the hell needs you anyway? I'll do it all myself. Enjoy your temple of solitude, asshole!"

And with that, I turned my back on him and stomped off.

6

I SLAMMED SHUT THE DOOR TO LARRY'S ROOM BEHIND ME and crossed to the nearest window, pulling the drapes aside to allow a bit of sunlight into the stuffy enclosure. Bill's jar rattled as I set it down none too gently upon a free patch of Larry's desk.

Bill looked at me, his brow furrowed and his lips bent into a frown. "Look, Lexie. I appreciate you thinking of me, but... I'm not sure I'm the one best situated to help you here."

Larry's bedroom was twice as large as mine, but you never would've known it from looking at it. The space was almost as tightly packed as the basement. Bookshelves covered nearly every square inch of wall. Larry had even positioned his bed in the center of the space to give himself more room for books.

I skirted a broad, hardwood table piled high with beakers, vials, leather pouches, bowls of crystals and bone fragments, a hot plate, and a pair of safety glasses, and stepped to the floor lamp hovering over Larry's bed. I flicked it on, sending a warm glow into the musty corners. "You may not be the best one to help, Bill, but at the moment you're the only one."

Bill pressed his lips together, rubbing what little saliva there was across his gangrenous skin. "That's the thing. You'd be better off going it alone. I don't know the first thing about magic."

"That's not true," I said as I returned to the desk, which was about half the size of the one in the living room that Larry normally conducted his business from. "You've spent more time than any of us around Larry. You've known him for, what? Fifteen years?"

"Almost seventeen," said Bill. "But that doesn't make me an expert on magic. That knowledge isn't passed along based on proximity, you know."

I stopped in front of his jar and crossed my arms. "How did you meet him?"

"I don't see how that—"

"How?"

Bill sighed and rolled his eyes. "Larry recovered me from a subterranean cave while spelunking as part of a field trip during his time at Zephyrburr Magical Academy."

"And then what did he do with you?"

"He kept me in his dorm room at the academy. Again, I don't see how this makes your point. Just because I spent time around wizards doesn't mean I know magic, much less that I'm capable of teaching it to you."

"I don't buy it," I said. "I've seen you use magic, regardless of what you call it. Your navigation abilities? You're clearly tapping into magical ley lines in the earth and using them to guide you. Just because you're not aware you're using magic doesn't mean you're not. And beyond that, you've partnered with Larry to become a conduit for magic. You led us to the

O'Neill's farm near Lockhart after Larry bewitched you to be able to key in on Benedict's demon stench."

"Exactly," said Bill. "That was *Larry's* spell. I had nothing to do with it. All I did was sniff the air and figure out what direction the funk was coming from."

I threw up my hands. "Come on, Bill! Work with me. You've been answering the phones. You know how many requests we've had from folks with magical problems, or at least problems that sound like they need a mystical touch to solve. Every day Larry stays in the basement, we're losing jobs, losing revenue. I don't want to scare you, but I went over our financials. We need the income. How am I supposed to keep this business afloat on a few weeks worth of magical training? I can't pack up and head off to Zephyrburr, even if I did show the appropriate level of ability. I need help!"

Bill's bluetooth headset twisted as he frowned. His skin wasn't the most elastic after centuries of undead decay, but a few lines nonetheless grew between his eyebrows. "What's going on with you and Larry? Whatever the beef is, I'm sure you can squash it."

"He doesn't want to work with me. It's that simple."

"Look, I get it. This disease is tough to accept. I didn't deal with it well, either, and I don't have anywhere near the willpower Larry does, but—"

"He doesn't want to work with me, Bill." I paused as I saw the hurt flash in Bill's eyes. I sighed. "Sorry. I'm on edge, for a lot of reasons, but Larry's not an option. He's not going to help with the business or with training me in any capacity anytime soon, so don't bother suggesting it."

Bill did that jiggle that suggested he was trying to shake his head. "Alright. Well, I don't know what use I can be to you, but... I'll do what I can. Whatever you need, we can bumble through it together. Just don't ask me to do anything that requires limbs."

I smiled, even though I didn't feel much joy. "Thanks. I appreciate it. And you don't have to worry about that. I'm mostly after knowledge. If nothing else, I was hoping you could help me navigate this mess of books." I waved at the shelves.

Bill flashed me his yellow chompers. "Well, navigation is one thing I'm good at."

"I know," I said. "The pun was intended."

"Sure it was. So what are you looking to learn? Elemental magic? Fire, lightning, ice? Or something more in the realm of enchantments? Or perhaps divinations?"

I paced around the central table, eyeing the magical supplies scattered haphazardly over the surface. I'd seen many of the same things at Nine Moons. Maybe the place wasn't a sham. "I don't need work on elemental magic. That's one of the few things I'm somewhat confident in."

Bill's eyebrow rose. "Really?"

I wouldn't have admitted it to anyone else, not Dawn, or Bill, and certainly not Larry given the circumstances, but I'd been practicing my skills every night. Every evening I sat down and cleared the space around me, not as a precaution but as a ritual to prepare myself for magic. It helped me clear my mind of distractions and allowed me to focus on the energies that flowed through me. As Larry had explained on more than one occasion, magic was like the Force, an energy that flowed around us, occupying a different dimension most of us weren't able to sense. Tapping into it required extreme concentration.

I closed my eyes and stretched out with my sixth sense. I felt a hum in the earth, a trickle of energy flowing through the air, through the table at my side, through the books and bookcases, up through the ground into my legs, my core, flowing to the tips of my fingers. It wasn't the torrent of energy I'd felt in the moments I'd shared the same body as Larry in the spirit world, but I could sense it. I knew it was there.

I flicked into the magical dimension, not with my fingers but with the new sense I'd been honing, grabbing ahold of the energy and funneling it into my fingers as I snapped.

I felt heat, and when I opened my eyes, a flicker of flame danced among my fingertips. I smiled. "See? No problem."

"Great," said Bill. "Now when one of us has a birthday party, we won't need to head to the kitchen for the lighter."

The flames died as I lost my grip on the energies. As they fled, so too did my self-confidence. "I mean... I think it's pretty neat."

Bill coughed and muttered. "Sorry. That was rude. I've spent so much time around Larry that being an asshole comes second nature. You should be proud."

"Thanks." The apology didn't lift my spirits.

"So... how much can you summon?" asked Bill. "Gouts? Infernos?"

I shrugged as I looked up at him. "It's a work in progress. Ice, too. I'm getting better."

He shuddered in the odd motion that I'd long since learned to interpret as a nod. "Good. So, what is it you're hoping to learn?"

I pushed the feelings of inadequacy down where they wouldn't show. "I need to learn tracking magic. That's something that could really help, in particular with the Nine Moons case."

Bill snorted. "Come on, girl. You've been around Larry long

enough to know there's no such thing. That's why I sent you to Nine Moons in the first place."

"Larry's full of shit," I said. "He either never learned how it works or he's gaslighting the rest of us by telling us it doesn't exist."

"How do you figure that?" asked Bill.

"He enchanted you to tap into his sense of magical Smell and was able to combine that with your intrinsic navigational sense to track down Benedict," I said. "Smell. Hearing. Sight. You've heard Larry talk about those, right? Basically beefed up versions of the traditional senses, enhanced by magic. Using those in a targeted manner to key in on a subject? That's tracking magic by any other name, and that's what I need to get better at."

"Well, I can walk you through the enchantment Larry cast on me before we went in search of Benedict," said Bill. "And I do remember Larry returning from his classes on Magical Scents and Sensibilities at Zephyrburr—that really was the name, by the way. If you act as my eyes, I bet I could help you find the texts he used."

I clapped my hands, my spirits lifting. "Now we're talking."

Bill's eyes veered to the shelves overflowing with thick tomes. "Might want to buckle in, though. It took Larry months to get a handle on this stuff, and that was with an experienced teacher, not a wisecracking portable card catalog."

"Good point," I said. "I'll get us some coffee. We're going to need it."

7

My head swam as I hunched over Larry's bedroom table. Formulas and instructions on how to properly dry and separate insect wings from their torsos floated across my field of vision. I shook my head and blinked them away, but even with them gone, I couldn't remember what stage of the process I was at. I'd already extracted the frog bone marrow, but was I supposed to mix it into the sycamore tea now or later?

I glanced at the assortment of bowls in front of me. "What do we do after we've steeped the sycamore bark in the hot water again?"

Only the tip of Bill's jar peeked over the enormous leather bound book I'd propped open in front of him. He couldn't turn the pages without my assistance, but the particular tome he gazed at had very small print. The entire potion we were working on fit on a single page. "You need to make sure the tea has been heated to boiling, then add it to the frog's leg extract slowly, folding the mixture gently to avoid losing the air bubbles that we already worked so hard to trap in it."

"*We*. Right." I turned the dial up on the hotplate, atop of which stood the beaker with water that had been stained a slight amber color from the bark.

"Are you saying I haven't helped?" said Bill. "Because I don't have to be here. I could be watching *Game of Thrones*, you know."

I forced myself not to ask how he managed to get ahold of the remote. "So I'm supposed to *fold* the extract in? Like egg whites into a soufflé?"

"I don't know. I guess. I don't do a lot of cooking."

I peered at the heavy book in front of Bill's jar. "You're sure it says fold?"

I couldn't see his eyes, but by the tone of his voice, I'm pretty sure he was glaring at me. "If *you'd* rather interpret these instructions, by all means, take the book. Seriously. I sprang for HBO's streaming service. Even if I get tired of Westeros, I could find something else to occupy my time with."

"You know I can't read ancient Greek," I said. "I'm still working on my Latin."

"Then stop questioning my translation," said Bill. "And no, I have no idea if the Greeks used the term folding the same way modern pastry chefs do. I may be able to stumble my way through the language, but that doesn't make me a historian."

"Just seems to me if we add boiling tea to the frothed frog's marrow, it's going to ruin all the work I already put in."

"Lexie..."

"Sorry. I'll shut my trap and follow instructions." I glanced around the table for a spatula. I seemed to be lacking one, but there was a wide, shallow spoon that could probably do the trick. "How much extract did you say again? Four grams?"

"Four *drams*, with a d."

"What the hell is a dram?"

"A unit of measurement, obviously," said Bill. "It was part of the apothecary's system. Pretty sure the ancient Greeks used it as a measure of weight, not volume, though."

"So how much does a dram weigh?"

"What do I look like, an encyclopedia? Check your phone."

I pulled the thing out of my pocket and thumbed through the web browser. "Wikipedia says the Greek drachma was a weight of six obols, one hundredth of a Greek mina, or about four point three seven grams. The drachma was a coin, though, not a unit of measurement."

"Coins and weights were the same thing in ancient times," said Bill. "If you needed to weigh out twenty drams of wheat, you could use the coins as a counterweight on a scale. That's part of the reason the punishment for scraping precious metal off the edge of a coin was to chop off the offender's hand."

"Really?" I asked.

"How the hell should I know? I told you I'm not a historian. I'm just making shit up."

I rolled my eyes as I pulled up my phone's calculator. "Alright. Let's see. Four point three seven times four gives... seventeen point four eight. Let's call it seventeen and a half. I don't think this scale goes down to less then tenths of a gram." Larry had an old timey balance scale on his table, but I'd brought the digital scale from the kitchen when we'd started. I put a small glass bowl atop it, zeroed the scale, and started scooping the frothed marrow with the wide spoon.

"Now be careful," said Bill as I measured the foamy concoction into the bowl. "The instructions say you'll need to add the powdered ox horn, dried gypsy moth wings, and Persian blue fine salt *immediately* after folding in the tea, otherwise it won't work."

I still didn't know how the heck I was supposed to fold boiling liquid into a foam. "And when you say it won't work, are we talking about a fizz and a poof and a dud or a flash and a bang and suddenly my eyebrows are missing?"

"You're asking me to read between the lines, Lexie."

"Well, you already made this mixture once before," I said. "I figured you'd have a little insight."

"Correction," said Bill. "*Larry* made the concoction and gave it to me. I had no role in the brewing of the potion. Besides, how would I know what happens if we screw it up? Larry executed the instructions correctly."

"Fair enough. How much of the dry ingredients?"

Bill gave me the amounts, in drams of course, which I converted to grams. Once I had all the ingredients measured, I combined them and checked on my sycamore bark tea. It boiled merrily on the hotplate.

"You still there?" asked Bill. "I'd like to see when you mix the final batch."

I crossed over and pulled the tome away from his line of sight. "Why? So you can laugh at me when I turn into a frog?"

"Just because there's frog's marrow in the tonic doesn't mean it'll turn you into an amphibian," said Bill. "I have faith in you."

I wasn't sure if he was being facetious or not, but I appreciated the vote of confidence. "Seems like it's go time."

Bill cocked an eyebrow at me. "Seems like it."

I edged back to the scale and the hotplate on the opposite side of the table. I didn't feel terribly comfortable with what I was about to do, but I soothed my fears by assuring myself that what I was doing wasn't magic, at least not in any sense that I was aware of. I wasn't tapping into the energies vibrating along a hidden dimensional plane, forcing them through my body to do my bidding. I was simply mixing ingredients. I was cooking, for all intents and purposes. What could go wrong?

I used an oven mitt to pick up the beaker of bubbling sycamore tea and grasped the wide spoon with the other. "Here goes nothing."

I'd already measured the liquids, so I started to pour. The hot tea steamed as it came into contact with the frothed marrow. As I expected, the foam I'd worked so hard to lighten immediately began to melt as the tea came into contact with it.

"Fold," said Bill. "Fold!"

"I'm folding!" I increased the speed at which I worked the spoon down and through the mixture, but I didn't want to go too fast either, otherwise I'd whip it rather than folding it. Then again, who knew what the ancient Greeks who wrote the potions text intended or even if Bill's translation had been a hundred percent accurate?

I think it was nerves more than anything that caused the speed of my folding to increase. Try as I might, I couldn't keep it from turning into a whip. Not that it mattered. The mixture was completely liquid as the last drops of tea poured from the beaker's lips.

"Quick! The powders!" called Bill.

I tossed the spoon to the table and scooped up the bowl with the ox horn, gypsy moth wings, and blue salt. I wanted to toss the mixture into the bubbling liquid and dive for cover in the event that the whole thing blew up into a cloud of blistering, acrid smoke, but I'd measured the ingredients down to the tenth of a gram for a reason. I couldn't risk half the powders slopping out of the bowl onto the table. Instead I reached as far as I could and brought my mitten clad hand up to my face to protect me from the worst of what might occur.

Surprisingly, nothing exploded. Not exactly, anyway. Sparks flew as the powder met the bubbling surface, not the sort of glowing yellow sparks you might get when you tossed a heavy log into a bed of hot coals, but rather a shower of glimmering purple ones, like a special effect at a drag musical. I heard a sizzling like that of pop rocks tossed in soda, and a sugary, smoky aroma filled the air, as if someone had basted a slab of barbecue chicken with Coca-Cola.

The purple sparkle shower died, and the popping fizzled away to nothing. I pulled my arm down and bent in closer. "Is that it?"

"It didn't kill you," said Bill. "It's a miracle!"

"You realize if I'd died, the blast probably would've taken you with me."

Bill smirked. "I mean, I'm already dead, so..."

I pulled the mitten from my hand and poked the bowl. The murky brown liquid rippled in a perfectly normal fashion. "So now what?"

"What do you mean, now what?" said Bill. "Now you drink it."

I grimaced. "All of it?"

"Well, when Larry gave it to me, he poured it in my jar, so I don't really know how much he used. You also weigh a lot more than me given that you have a body and all. Just take a big swig."

I frowned. "But... it's got frog bone marrow and moth wings in it."

"Like that's the worst thing you've put in your body," said Bill. "You're a college student. If someone put grain alcohol in it and offered it as punch at a rager, you'd drink your weight in it."

"That's a thought. Can we add booze? I think we have a nice bourbon in the kitchen."

"Oh, for crying out loud. Drink it."

I picked up the bowl, which was still warm to the touch but not as hot as I'd expected. Maybe some of the energy had been lost in the shimmering purple sparks.

Steeling myself, I lifted the bowl to my lips, closed my eyes, and tipped it back.

The concoction was bitter, salty, and slightly tangy, but barely had the tastes registered before my eyes snapped open. They weren't the only thing. My sinuses flared, as did my nostrils, and suddenly everything around me felt incredibly *alive*.

"Whoa. WHOA." I blinked and shook my head, but the sheer barrage of sensory information flowing into me wouldn't slow. "Holy crap! It's like I swallowed a spoonful of wasabi and snorted coke at the same time."

"Yeah, it's got a kick to it," said Bill. "I probably should've warned—wait, you've done coke?"

"I mean, it's like how I figured it would feel. From watching movies and stuff." I spun, taking in every inch of the room. Suddenly, I felt like I could see into the nooks and crannies that darkness had previously covered. A tingle rippled through my muscles, a jittery feeling of adrenaline, excitement, and excess sugar. I felt like I couldn't close my eyes, couldn't blink, but it was the potion's intended effect that really rocked me on my heels.

I'd learned how to use my Smell a few weeks ago. I'd first felt it while tracking Benedict. His evil, putrid aroma was so potent even someone as unskilled as me had been able to pick it out from the magical background, but since then, I'd struggled with the sense. Larry claimed it came naturally, but magic circles, hexes, enchanted weapons, and supernatural creatures—I couldn't smell any of them.

Until now.

I couldn't explain how, but everything magical suddenly had an additional shape to it. It wasn't a visible shape either, as they remained even when I was finally able to close my eyes. Faint musty outlines traced the edges of the books lining the walls. The bowls and utensils and ingredients scattered across the table before me showed as indistinct masses of colored mist, some cold, some hot, others pungent or earthy. In a way, the information felt visual, but it wasn't, just an interpretation of the magical scents I could finally detect transformed into a signal my brain could process. I also knew it wasn't visual data because I could smell beyond the walls of Larry's room. The hunched form of Tank in his room on the other side of the first floor, faintly sweaty and wild, the werebear portion of him more obvious than ever. The cracked remains of the demon tooth Larry had enchanted for me that I kept for sentimental reasons which smelled old and dangerous. A host of strange scents coming from the basement, including the putrid scent of Larry himself. That one didn't smell particularly different from his actual scent.

I smiled as I turned my attention toward Bill. "I can't believe it worked."

He smiled back. "For your next birthday, I'm going to get you one of those Believe in Yourself posters. One with a cat on a tree branch."

"How long do the effects last?"

Bill wiggled in the way he did in lieu of shrugging. "Hard to say. It was between twenty-four and forty-eights hours for me, but I had a different dose than you did. Who knows? Maybe it won't wear off at all. You're still working on honing your magical skills after all. It's possible you'll master the art, same as Larry has."

I could only hope, as distracting as the newfound ability might be. The uses for it would be limitless. Still...

I grabbed my phone. "Sorry to leave you hanging, Bill, but I've got to go. Can't waste this potion while it's got its hooks in me. I'll see you later."

Bill's voice dogged me as I darted out of Larry's bedroom. "Aw, come on. At least move me back to the living room! Westeros, Lexie. *Westeros!*"

8

My Suburban rumbled as I pulled up in front of Nine Moons Witch Supply. I turned the headlights off as I killed the engine, but the warm, yellow glow of the halogen lights overlooking the strip mall's parking lot still illuminated enough of the shop for me to see.

"Aw, come on." I undid my seatbelt and hopped out of the truck, skipping to the front door. Sure enough, the lights inside were all off, and when I tested the front door it was locked.

I checked the hours printed on the front of the glass. Open 9 AM to 7 PM, it said. I pulled my phone from my pocket and gaped when I saw the time. 10:30? When the hell had it gotten so late?

I looked around me, for the first time seeing past the magical aura that infused so many of the objects around me. The skies had darkened, and the air had cooled to less than the traditional Texas summer swelter. Had I really spent all afternoon and half the evening preparing the potion with Bill? And how in the world had I not noticed night had fallen on my ride over from the house? I'd been half joking about the cocaine thing, but maybe the magical potion I'd consumed was more of a drug than I'd realized.

My body vibrated with unspent energy, as if I'd pounded a six pack of Red Bulls. I didn't want to wait until morning to solve mysteries. I wanted to do it now! Not to mention I didn't know how long the effects of the tonic would last. Bill had said up to two days, but what did he know? He was just a head in a jar. Plus apparently the thing hadn't affected him the same way. Maybe I'd put something into the tincture Larry hadn't, or I'd used a different recipe than Larry had. Why wouldn't Bill have warned me about that? Christ, my mind was racing a mile a minute. And where was Augusta? Oh, it was after hours. Right. I shook the door in the frame. "Come on. Rats!"

I harrumphed as I headed back to my truck. I jumped inside and turned the key in the ignition, barely remembering to close my door before I did so. The truck lurched as I put it in reverse, then again as I cranked on the wheel and put it in drive. Jesus, had I driven all the way over here so recklessly? I'd been lucky not to get pulled over. Little chance I could convince a police officer I wasn't drunk, at least not until they gave me a breatha-lyzer test. Not that it would help. If they thought I was acting abnormally and failed, they'd assume I was high on something more illegal than booze. Heroin. Meth. Hell, maybe they'd think I'd been pounding cough syrup.

I slapped myself and shook my head. "Focus, Lexie. You're here to investigate. You're a witch. Don't let the potion get the best of you."

I cranked on the wheel as I headed around the edge of the strip mall, barely remembering to turn the headlights back on as I delved into the poorly illuminated service section in the back. Augusta said her back door had remained locked during her break-in, but I hadn't exited through it during my time in the store. I didn't know what it looked like. Probably like the back of any store in a strip mall. Lots of pavement. Maybe some dumpsters. A door. Jeez, Lexie, of course there's going to be a door. Which store was it from the end? Fourth? Fifth? I remembered seeing a Vietnamese food place and a discount shoe store as I'd driven past. Maybe third?

I leaned over my steering wheel, gripping it tight as I peered into the gloom. Which back entrance was it? That dumpster smelled like pho. Probably not that one, then. Then I saw it. Past the solid wall of concrete that comprised the rear of the outdoor mall, magical auras swirled around the junk in Augusta's back room. A bunch of colors and shapes, all different sizes and strengths, too. Guess she hadn't been lying. She did sell witch supplies. Even after she'd shown us the goods I'd doubted her. Why hadn't I noticed the auras when I first stepped outside my Suburban in the front? I guess I had, but I hadn't focused on them.

I slapped myself again as I put the Suburban in park. "Christ. Get it together, Lexie. For real this time."

I hopped out of my truck and closed the door behind me. The glowing auras of the magical doodads in Augusta's shop shimmered in the darkness, mixing together into a jumbled mass of Smells that slapped me with its intensity. I blinked and snorted, trying to focus on what I could see with my own two eyes. I'd need to practice using my newfound magical Smell in conjunction with my other senses lest one get overwhelmed by the other. Since I didn't want to bang a shin into a wayward trashcan, I pulled my phone from my pocket and turned on the flashlight.

Good thing my mom didn't raise a dummy. All sorts of junk

had been piled up outside the backdoor to Nine Moons, very little of which looked like surplus wares or garbage. Four or five large crates, each of them painted black and with the words "Property of BSI" printed across the sides sat next to the exterior wall. Had Otis and Jane left them there? They might've been able to fit one of them in their Escalade, but not four. I wondered what was in them. They looked like they were large enough to transport live animals or heavy munitions, neither of which gave me a warm and fuzzy feeling inside.

I skirted them as I made my way to the back door. With my phone still in hand, I tested the handle. It was locked. I cursed. On the one hand, it was nice that Augusta had locked her store. It didn't prove she'd done it on the night of the break-in, but finding the door unlocked would've poked a giant hole in her story. Still, having the thing locked didn't help me now. I'd hoped to investigate the crime scene with my newfound spidey-sense, but it wouldn't do me much good if I couldn't get close to the mauled herbs and tussled graduation gowns.

Or would it? Thinking of my magically-enhanced olfactory ability as a superpower actually made a lot of sense. Spider-Man couldn't see through walls, but he could detect danger, get a sense of where it was coming from and when. Why couldn't I use my powers in the same way? The colorful, fuzzy masses that swam in my vision were proof that I could, even if the scents were muddled into an indiscernible jumble. There were hints of herbaceous scents, floral scents and mild, milky ones, sweet ones tinged with lemon and allspice, cold scents of metal and desiccated wood, scents of rot and decay and the passage of time, scents of heat and danger and other things that shouldn't have scents but did, and a few stinky scents that reminded me of nothing with an earthly analog.

I took a deep breath and let it out slowly. "You've got to focus, Lexie. Third time's the charm. Be like Spider Gwen. *Be Spider Gwen.*"

I turned off my phone's flashlight and closed my eyes. I focused on my heartbeat, ignoring the jittery tremor that rushed through my veins thanks to the moth wing and tree bark potion. Feel the beat. *Thump thump. Thump thump.* There is is. Count it out. One one thousand. Two one thousand. Three one thousand.

I wasn't sure how long I stood there, focusing on nothing but my heartbeat. Maybe a minute, probably not more than two. But with my eyes shut tight and my chin tucked against my chest, the flood of sensory information from my eyes and ears and nose dimmed. The world quieted around me. Clean air flowed in and out of my nostrils, and darkness enveloped me—all except the glows provided by my newfound sixth sense.

I tipped my head up without opening my eyes, casting my Smell past the locked door into the back of Augusta's shop. All the Smells were still there, but I could get a sense of each one's direction. The lemony one to the right, a few paces inside the door, the rotten one far away and to the left, and the herbaceous ones perhaps ten or fifteen paces in front of me.

Those would be the scents from Augusta's grow operation. Without moving, I envisioned myself stepping forward into the space I'd found myself in earlier this afternoon, surrounded by the hogweed and periwinkle and whatever else she had in there. I placed myself among the plants, feeling their scents around me, not sure which was which but nonetheless able to pick one from another. One to my right that smelled of lemongrass, another to my left that reminded me of sage, each with a unique color to their auras. Where was the rack that had been destroyed? Ah, the space devoid of scents in front of me. I reached out with my magical sense toward the patch of dirt on Augusta's floor. I'd expected the mound to smell earthy. Instead, as I keyed in on the soil, all I could detect was a faint Smell of... *licorice.*

I opened my eyes, suddenly whisked out of Augusta's shop and back to the steps outside her door. Was the scent meaningful? As far as I knew, non-magical things shouldn't have magical scents. The fact that the earth had an aroma meant there was something magical about it, didn't it? Then again, the herbs on Augusta's shelves had magical auras as well, and they were just plants. Or were they? Maybe everything had a magical signature.

I sighed. Navigating my way through the bold new world of magic would've been a hell of a lot easier with Larry at my side, but that simply wasn't an option at the moment. For now, I'd have to do it myself and follow the leads wherever they took me.

So... licorice. Maybe it was nothing, but maybe it was a clue. I closed my eyes again and keyed in on my heartbeat. This time it was easier. In only ten or twenty seconds, I found myself immersed in the scents around me. I reached out, searching for the faint but familiar scent of sweet and tangy black candy. Augusta had said her supposed intruder had made their way around the back of the shop, getting not just into the herbs but also the clothes and her potion supplies. If the licorice Smell had anything to do with them and not merely the soil, it stood to reason I might find the Smell elsewhere. Unfortunately, I hadn't looked around the rest of the storage space in back with Dawn so I didn't know where to cast my attention. Instead, I stumbled around the space, casting my Smell this way and that without any real sense of what I was doing, all while searching for the licorice Smell I'd found among the displaced earth. Was that it? Over by a wall that smelled of old books and fresh leather? Maybe not. Darn, the scent was so faint...

I gave up after a minute or two. If the licorice scent was anywhere else in Augusta's shop, I couldn't sense it, at least not among all the other magical Smells accosting me.

I blinked, suddenly feeling stupid. I didn't need to pick the scent out of a bouquet of other magical aromas. I needed to pick it out from a clean, untainted background. The whole reason I'd crafted the Smell potion was to turn myself into a magical bloodhound and prove Larry wrong about his whole 'tracking magic doesn't exist' mantra. That meant tracking the licorice scent *outside* Augusta's shop.

I turned, descended the steps, and headed past the Brute Squad crates. I ignored the shop behind me, instead reaching out with my senses into the parking lot. If someone broke through the Nine Moons back door, they must've driven along the same path I had. I paused in the middle of the asphalt, focusing on the route I'd taken, but after a minute of standing there, breathing as I focused on my heartbeat, I couldn't detect even the faintest hint of licorice. I turned and tried the same thing along the back of the strip mall in the other direction. A minute later, I sighed in frustration.

Either I'd been wrong about the scent, or whoever broke into Augusta's place hadn't driven up. I refused to admit that I didn't know how to properly use my magical Smell yet, so I tried to think of other ways someone might've approached and busted into Nine Moons. Maybe they'd flown in? A sprite could've swooped by, maybe through the air vents. They were small. Either that... or someone just walked up.

I paused at the edge of the asphalt behind the strip mall.

The lights from the mall parking lot cast a pale glow that died at my feet, but I'd been in the darkness long enough for my eyes to adjust. The earth sloped down to a sewer main and a flat expanse of concrete that would turn into a retention pond during a central Texas downpour. Beyond that, dark woods loomed ominously, not a scrap of artificial light creeping through them.

I climbed down the slope, walked across the concrete, and stopped at the edge of the trees. I closed my eyes one more time and focused on my magical Smell, reaching out with it, searching, probing. I caught a snippet of a plant here and there, wild versions of whatever Augusta had in her store, but nothing else. And then...

I wrinkled my nose. Was I imagining it, or was there a hint of licorice in the air?

Without letting go of the sensory thread, I turned the flashlight on my phone back on and stepped into the woods. I tried to follow the scent, but it was so nebulous and faint I couldn't track it. Instead I stumbled forward, casting my phone's light around in search of anything out of the ordinary. On first glance, it looked like any other forest at night—dark, vaguely creepy, with leaves and debris crackling underfoot with each of my steps. I tried looking for signs that someone had been through it—broken branches, damaged bark, other stuff I'd learned from watching the occasional episode of *Survivorman* with my dad—but between it being dark and me not being much of an outdoorswoman, I didn't have any success.

Just when I was about to turn back, I noticed a glimmer of an aura and caught with it a whiff of licorice. I stepped forward, weaving around a thorny bush to get closer to it. It was in the soil, same as the scent I'd caught at Nine Moons. My foot squelched in a patch of wet earth as I bent closer to the spot, and I moved my flashlight over the area to give myself a glimpse of what was there.

It was a footprint—at least, I think it was. The thing had ill-defined edges, but there were segmented portions to it, with deeper imprints of what I assumed was a heel and the ball of a foot. Regardless of what had left it, one thing was clear. The footprint was *BIG*. Shaquille O'Neal's older, larger brother sort of big.

I gulped as the tremor from the magical potion drained out of me, replaced instead with a sudden existential dread. For the first time, it dawned on me that I was alone in the woods, tracking something that might've been much larger, more dangerous, and wild than I'd ever considered, using magic I didn't fully understand, and without having told anyone where I was.

Perhaps I'd be better served returning tomorrow with someone at my side. As I took one last glance at the footprint, I was sure of it. Without looking back, I turned tail and ran toward my truck.

9

I yawned and turned over in bed, cracking my eyes to check on the alarm clock. It was only eight, but the sun already streamed through my window, as bright as if it were noon. I thought about going back to sleep, but with the will of a seasoned athlete, I pulled myself out of bed, threw some shorts on underneath my Texas Softball tee, and headed downstairs.

I stumbled into the kitchen, feeling groggy. The tingle of last night's potion had faded, as had its effects, but they hadn't disappeared entirely. I could still see auras of magical artifacts at the edges of my vision, as well as smell the strange scents of objects in Larry's room and upstairs and even in the storage shed outside. I grabbed a box of Frosted Mini-Wheats and filled a bowl when I caught a magical whiff of something coming from the basement, a putrid mix of rotten fruit and white male resentment. It wasn't a normal smell, but it left a sour taste in my mouth nonetheless. Perhaps like smell and taste, Smell was also tied to the more traditional senses.

I pushed the cereal box back onto the counter and opted for a mug of coffee instead. With that in hand, warming my throat and strengthening my synapses, I headed toward the living room. I'd barely walked in before Bill hailed me.

"There you are," he said. "About time you woke up."

I blinked at him as I took a sip of the coffee. I didn't say anything.

"Hello?" Bill lifted a ragged eyebrow at me. "You are awake, right?"

"Getting there," I said. "Give me a minute."

Bill still had his bluetooth headset in. I don't think he ever took it out. I suppose it wasn't easy for him to do it on his own. "Well, hurry it up. We've got places to go. People to see. Or at least you do."

I crossed to Larry's enormous desk. With him having moved into the basement, it would make sense to store it, maybe in the shed in back if it would fit. Probably would send Larry into convulsions if we tried. Then again, if it got him out of the basement and forced him to interact with the rest of us...

I sat on the corner of the pine, next to the side table where Bill preferred to keep his jar. "Is there a reason for your sense of urgency? We're not under attack are we? I would've heard Tank's roar by now if that were the case."

Bill drew himself up to his full nine inches. "My urgency is rooted in professionalism and concern for this business. We've already gotten another three calls this morning. Add that to the backlog of cases we've acquired over the last week and a half, and yeah, I'd say we have better things to do than sleep in."

"Easy for you to say. You're dead. You don't sleep."

"Which is a cruel joke, if you ask me," said Bill. "That whole you can sleep when you're dead bit? Lies and slander, all of it."

I glanced at a pile of mail next to Bill. I gave him a nod. "You bring that in?"

Bill frowned. "Very funny. Dawn brought it in before heading out for her morning jog."

I picked up the envelope on top. It was postmarked from our mortgage lender. The words PAST DUE were splattered across the front in red ink. "I'm guessing you didn't open any of these."

"Also funny," said Bill.

"But you saw who sent them."

Bill's lip curled down. "I mean, it's sitting right next to me..."

I sighed. Now I understood Bill's urgency. "Look, I went over everything with Dawn yesterday. I'll admit, our money situation doesn't look great, but we're hanging in there."

Bill tunneled into me with worried eyes. "It says third and final notice on the envelope, Lexie."

So it did. "I'll cash the checks from the two jobs we finished yesterday. They didn't bring much, but anything will help. What other calls did you get this morning? Anything a wannabe witch with a barely functional knowledge of magic can tackle on her own?"

"Don't sell yourself short, Lexie," said Bill. "Last night's potion worked, or at least I assume it did based on the speed with which you ran out of Larry's bedroom. Speaking of which, I had to get Dawn to put me back on my table."

I didn't take the bait. "Give it to me straight. Can I tackle any of the jobs we have lined up on my own?"

Bill did that shimmy shrug thing. "I mean... maybe?"

I shook my head, as frustrated with my magical ineptitude as with the situation. "You said Dawn went out for a run?"

"She did."

"Guess that leaves me one option." I set my coffee on the desk and headed toward the stairs, hooking a right toward the front of the house. I stopped before the closed door to Tank's room.

I knocked on the hardwood. "Tank? It's me, Lexie. We need to talk."

I waited a few moments, but Tank didn't respond. I tried again. "Seriously, Tank. I know you've had a rough couple weeks, but you can't stay like this forever. Let me in so we can chat."

Still nothing. I pressed my ear against the door to see if I could detect any snoring or heavy breathing. I failed to hear any, so I reached out with what was left of my Smell. I'd picked up on Tank's aura yesterday, a sweaty, wild aroma I'd expected from a werebear. I sensed nothing.

I tested the door handle and found it unlocked. I twisted and pushed, poking my head into the room. "Tank?"

Tank's room was messier than the last time I'd seen it. His bedsheets were rumpled, the top sheet cast to the foot of his bed and the fitted sheet hanging onto his mattress by a thin elastic strap. Empty soda bottles and energy bar wrappers overflowed from the wastebasket beside his desk, which in turn was covered with pieces of mail, dirty dishes, and discarded clothes. The blinds over the window had been closed as tightly as they'd go, casting the room into a deep gloom, and a stale body odor hung in the air. Of Tank, there was no sign.

I opened the door to let the room air out and returned to the living room. I gave Bill a nod. "Have you seen Tank?"

"He was banging around late last night," said Bill. "He's not in his room?"

"Nope. I figured he'd be asleep. I thought that was all he'd been doing these last two weeks. I can't do all these jobs on my own. I need his help, on the Nine Moons job if nothing else."

The back door creaked. I about-faced, figuring to find Dawn returning from her jog. Instead, it was Tank who stumbled inside and closed the door behind him.

"Speak of the devil," I said.

Tank was huge, maybe six foot six and close to three hundred pounds, but very little of it was bad weight. With smooth, symmetrical features, dark eyes, and chocolate skin that had the faintest hint of gloss to it, he was quite easy on the eyes, especially when he took his shirt off. He wasn't looking so hot today, though. He wore a pair of sweatpants and a moth-eaten T-shirt, the sort of stuff he threw on after ripping his regular clothes in an unplanned transformation. Dark sunglasses shrouded his eyes. A bit of beard scruff laced his cheeks, and he walked with a hunch and a deliberateness to his step that suggested he wasn't feeling so great.

He slowly turned toward me. "What?"

I sniffed the air, my Smell overpowered by the regular kind. He reeked of alcohol. "I said, speak of the devil. I've been trying to find you. Have you been drinking?"

Tank cringed as I talked. "Christ, Lexie. Not so loud."

"I'm speaking at a normal volume. Jesus, Tank, how much have you had? You realize it's eight in the morning, right? Have you even slept?"

Tank gritted his teeth and held the side of his head. "Can we do this some other time? Whatever this is about, it can wait."

"It can't, actually," I said. "Did you know the Nyte Patrol is underwater? Because we are, and part of the reason is because you and Larry have been moaning and groaning and refusing to do anything to help the rest of us for the past two weeks. We've got work to do—lots of it—and here you are, drunk as a skunk at breakfast time."

Tank pushed past me, headed toward the stairs. "I can't deal with this right now. I need to lie down."

Anger rose inside me, but I pushed it down with forced empathy. I didn't know what Tank was going through. I'd never lost someone as close to me as he had. Maybe I would've retreated into booze same as him if it happened to me.

I darted after him and grabbed him by the sleeve. "Tank, please. I know you're hurting, but we need your help. We're swamped, and last time I checked you were still part of this team. I can't pretend to understand what it's like to lose someone like Kiara, but—"

Tank bristled at the mention of his ex-wife's name. He ripped his sleeve from my grip with a powerful tug. "I said, NOT NOW!"

The man took two giant steps into his room and slammed the door behind him, leaving me alone in the hall with a mix of emotions washing through me: anger, regret, embarrassment.

As usual, anger won out. "Fine! Be that way. Guess I'll be doing everything on my own. *Again!*"

10

My Suburban rumbled as I drove down North Lamar. Austin may have been a hands-free city, but despite having bought Bill a bluetooth headset, I still didn't have one myself. Instead, I punched numbers into my phone, switched it to speaker, and dumped it in the console as soon as it started ringing.

This time, someone finally answered. Dawn spoke, her breath ragged and crackling through the speaker. "Hey. What's up?"

"There you are," I said. "Nice of you to finally pick up."

"I was out for a run." Dawn's heavy breathing confirmed she was telling the truth. "Didn't Bill tell you?"

"He did, I just figured you would've been home twenty minutes ago. Did you run a half-marathon?"

I heard a whirr of gears and a series of crystalline clunks. Ice being dispensed from a refrigerator door. "More of a ten K. What's going on?"

"What's going on is we've got work to do," I said. "Bill had taken three new calls when I talked to him earlier. I'm surprised he didn't mention it to you before you ran out the door."

Water gurgled through a faucet. "What makes you think he didn't?"

"So you're saying you're aware of how much work we have on our plates and you still skipped out for an hour and twenty minute run?"

"I clocked in at under an hour, thank you," said Dawn.

"My deepest apologies for slighting you. You're missing the point, though."

There was a pause on the line as Dawn greedily slurped ice cold water. "Maybe you could put the claws away and just tell me what's going on?"

I took a deep breath to calm my nerves. It didn't help. "What's going on is that we got an urgent looking notice from the bank about our mortgage, I completely failed to impress upon Larry or Tank the seriousness of our financial situation, resulting in both of them hating me even more, and I'm literally drowning beneath a pile of work that I'm totally unqualified for."

"You mean metaphorically, not literally."

"*Dawn!*"

"Sorry. What do you need from me, Lexie?"

A light turned yellow in front of me, and I hit the gas. I skated through as it turned red. "Bill split up the jobs. I've got a list I'm tackling as we speak. You should take the Hernandez and Wilson cases, as well as the one from the supernatural animal rehabilitation facility. They seemed more suited to your skillset than mine."

"Are you already on the road?"

"Of course I'm on the road," I said. "We'll never deal with

all these clients by sticking together. It's the only chance we have of working through the backlog."

"How am I supposed to get to any of these jobs then?"

I had the only car in the crew, and beyond that, Dawn had a phobia about driving. Apparently, growing up in Manila had caused deep-seated traffic related anxiety. Given how much of a badass she was about everything else, it was nice to know she had some weaknesses. "Just call an Uber or something."

"Are you sure about that?" she said. "I thought we were trying to save money, not balloon our expense account. Plus they don't like it when I bring my swords in their cars."

My phone buzzed as another call came in. I glanced at the console to check on the caller ID. It was my mom. *Damnit.*

"We'll write it off," I said. "Look, I have another call I have to take. Help me out with this, please?"

I heard her sigh. "Sure. I'll figure it out."

"Thanks, Dawn. Talk to you later." I took my eyes off the road for a second as I passed the last of the Shoal Creek greenbelt to tap the call switch button. As I heard the click of the call transferring, I hesitated for a moment. "Uh. Hey, mom."

My mother's warm voice bounced off the bottom of the console into my ear, less breathy than Dawn's. *"Hola, mi amor.* How are you doing?"

It was a loaded question. Fact of the matter was I hadn't spoken to my folks much since the showdown with Benedict. In the aftermath of dealing with the undead demon spirit, I'd called my parents to explain to them that our family cat, Mr. Whiskers, hadn't really been possessed, at least not by anything evil. I'd done it in an attempt to warn them about the actual demonic spirit who'd been coming to violently murder them. Of course, an integral part of my explanation about Mr. Whisker's behavior had been to explain to my deeply religious and not at all mystically-conscious parents that instead of taking an internship with a local engineering firm for the summer, I'd joined a group of supernatural guns for hire, discovered that magic was real, and decided to learn how to use it myself.

They hadn't taken it particularly well. In fact, I hadn't spoken with my mom in over a week. While that wouldn't have been anything of note with regards to my dad, it was a rare occurrence indeed for communication with my mom to be so limited.

Then again, perhaps my mother hadn't meant anything by asking how I was doing. Maybe she'd used it in the casual sense. "I'm doing okay. Busy, but all in all, pretty good. How about you?"

My mom sounded uncertain. "That's good... I guess. Is this a bad time?"

"No, not at all." I didn't want to turn my mother away, even if I was overwhelmed. Not calling had been my fault as much as hers. "I just have a lot on my plate at the moment. The phones have been ringing twenty four seven since word of our Benedict takedown made the rounds, which is a blessing and a curse. On the bright side, you can't run a successful business without business. On the other hand, I've had a lot more responsibility than I expected dumped into my lap, and Larry hasn't been willing to train me ever since we, ah... finished that last mission." I hadn't told my mom I'd turned him into a zombie. That might be the last straw.

My mom's voice was strained when she replied. "That's nice, *hija mia*. How about school? And softball? How are the girls doing?"

I frowned as I turned onto West 34th. "Well, I'm not taking

any summer classes, so school's not really going *at all* at the moment. That's one of the nice parts about summer, mom. And it's only been a few weeks since the end of the softball season. We won't start practices until the fall."

"Well, I know that, *bella*, but I figured you might've spent some time with Heather and Morgan and some of the other girls. At least I'd hoped you might've. At your age, summer is a time for having fun with your friends. Gaining new experiences. Not being focused on work all the time."

I glanced at my phone as I headed into the Bryker Woods subdivisions east of Mopac. "What are you talking about? Just a month ago all you could talk about was the engineering internship I'd told you I'd secured."

My mother's voice cooled a couple degrees, same as it always did when she felt she'd been called out. "Well, it would've been a nice stepping stone. It certainly would've been something to work hard for. It could've led to a nice job. A career after you finish school."

"Implying that the Nyte Patrol isn't worth busting my butt over?"

Any warmth that had been in my mother's voice disappeared. "Alexis, you know as well as I do that what you're doing isn't sustainable. All this magic and witches and werewolves business—even if any of it is real, it's not something you can stake your hopes and dreams and financial stability on."

"*If* it's real? Mom, you were there when I took hold of Mr. Whiskers. You saw him turn into a frenzied ball of pentagram-drawing craziness. Magic and all that supernatural stuff is very much real."

My mother sighed. "I don't want to fight you over this,

Alexis. You know it hurt your *papa* and *abuela* to hear this nonsense. I'm the one reaching out. I'm the one—"

"You're the one still doubting me," I said. "You won't believe what you saw with your own eyes, even after I explained to you everything that happened, even after I explained to you what Larry and Dawn and Tank are capable of."

"All I know is what you've told me, and honestly, they sound untrustworthy. I'm not sure you can believe anything these people are telling you. It concerns me that you moved in with them, given how little you know about them. The safe choice, the *smart* choice, would've been—"

The Suburban shuddered as I took a turn too fast. "The *smart* choice? Are you saying you raised a stupid daughter?"

"Alexis Mirabelle Rodriguez. Escúchame. No me hables así."

She'd busted out the Spanish. Now I knew she was upset. Unfortunately for both of us, so was I. "No, you listen. I'm not going to sit here while you passively-aggressively question my life choices. Magic is real. It's around you, it's around me, and more importantly, it's inside me. It's part of who I am. Another part of who I am is a member of the Nyte Patrol. Larry, Dawn, and Tank are my friends, even if you don't care for them. It doesn't mean I don't keep in touch with Heather or Morgan or anyone else, it just means I'm gaining new friends. Having fun with them, and having new experiences, which I'm apparently supposed to be doing now that it's summer time, assuming I'm not working a *real* job where all my hard work actually makes a difference."

My mother sighed. "Alexis. Don't be like this. You know that's not what I meant."

I pulled the Suburban onto the small cul-de-sac that housed the first of my clients for the day. "No, mom. I don't know that,

because everything you've said over the past two weeks has reinforced *exactly* what you've meant." I put the truck into park and
reached for the phone, my heart aching as my thumb hovered
over the screen. "Look, I've got to go. I've got work to do. I'll call
you later."

I hit the end call button before my mom could get another
word in. It was a rude thing to do, but I figured it would hurt
even more to let her keep going. Getting work done in my
current condition would be hard enough as it was.

11

THE HOME I'D PULLED UP IN FRONT OF WAS A MISHMASH of central Texas styles. The house itself was a small ranch with brick exterior and a detached carport, the sort of place that had been built for cheap in the late seventies and had ballooned in value in the decades since. The landscaping was decidedly more eco-chic, though. Broad swaths of smooth river stones separated the razor sharp pampas grasses from the smaller but no less dangerous cacti planted in the front. A raised vegetable bed sat next to a several hundred gallon corrugated metal cistern, one that was attached to the home's gutters by a fat pipe. As I got out of my car, I detected a whiff of decay. As I walked up the gravel path to the house, I noticed the compost tumbler next to the garden.

I took a deep breath as I rang the doorbell. My heart still beat hard in my chest from the exchange with my mom, and I hoped my cheeks weren't flushed. I wanted to present a professional image. Heck, I'd even put on my nice jeans and a blouse.

I heard some snippets of conversation before the clack of the latch. The door opened to about the three-quarter mark. A guy with short hair and a trim beard in his mid to late thirties stood there in a long sleeve Brooks Brothers dress shirt. He nodded at me as he spoke into the cell phone that he held against his ear. "—yeah, I'd suspect we'll need to order thirty of them from the supplier. We'll have to run it by our warehouse manager. Give me a sec here, Wayne. Can I help you?"

"Hi," I said. "I'm Lexie Rodriguez. With the Nyte Patrol. Are you Mr. Moore?"

He nodded and waved me in, pointing toward his living room as he continued to talk on the phone. "Yeah. That's right. Sorry, Wayne, what was that? Yeah, by Thursday at the latest I think. I'll be on site tomorrow. Maybe later tonight, depending on connections. I'm hoping to bump the flight up." The guy pointed at the living room again as I stood there in his entryway.

I nodded and moved out of his sphere of interaction. The living room was minimalist, with only a couple white, low-backed couches and a glass coffee table in front of the wall-mounted flatscreen. From my spot by the couch, I had a clear line of sight into the kitchen. I saw glossy cabinets, a broad marble island, and a Viking range. Clearly, the place had been remodeled. They didn't build them like this in the seventies.

Mr. Moore droned on behind me. I didn't pay much attention to the conversation other than to have a general idea of where he was. I crossed to the window and peered into the garden, eyeing a zucchini plant with leaves like small umbrellas. As I wondered what the oval-shaped plant beside it was—chard, maybe?—I heard footsteps and the voice grew. "I'll call you back as soon as I can. Yeah. Alright. Bye."

I turned to see Moore tucking his phone into his pants. "Hey. Sorry about that. Work. It's a constant endeavor, lately. Can I get you a water? Coffee?"

I waved him off. "No, I'm fine. Thank you, Mr. Moore."

"You can call me Gary." He pointed at the couch. "So where do you want to do it? Here? Or do you need to clear a space out? I'm not really sure how you guys operate even though I do business in the field, you know?"

Unfortunately, I didn't know, because I had no idea what Gary was talking about. Once again, Bill hadn't prepared me for the work he'd sent me out to tackle. I guess part of it was my fault for running into things headfirst, but I nonetheless reminded myself to have a chat with the talking zombie head about mission briefings.

"I'm sorry," I said. "We've got someone new answering phones. What is it you needed again?"

Gary smiled. "Don't sweat it. I'm usually working a half dozen jobs myself. All part of the hustle, right? I called to get a glyph of protection."

I blinked. *"A glyph of protection?"*

"That's right." Gary started rolling up his sleeves. "I'm heading into Brazil on business later today. My company contracts with some of the *brujas* who live on the border with Venezuela. We have a close relationship with a few, but there are lot of rival tribes in the Amazon, and given the geopolitical situation down there, things can get dicey, even beyond magic. That deep in the jungle, you can run into armed militant gangs, too, hence the glyph. Better safe than sorry, right?"

I ran my tongue across the back of my teeth, trying to keep a cool exterior. "Right."

"So, the couches," said Gary. "Do we need to move them? They're not that heavy, but I'll ask for your help, if you don't mind. The floor is alder, and I don't want to scratch it."

I paused, a single finger held in the air. I didn't know what to say, so I went with an oldie but a goodie. "Do you mind if I use your restroom first?"

"Oh. Sure." Gary pointed down the hallway. "Second door on your left."

I forced a smile. "Thanks."

I disappeared down the hall, shut the bathroom door behind me, and turned the faucet on to drown out the sound, even though I didn't think Mr. Moore was listening. I ripped my phone from my pocket and hit the speed dial for the house.

The phone rang twice before Bill answered. "You've reached the Nyte Patrol, paranormal consulting, wizarding services, and supernatural security, at your service. My name is Bill. How can I help you?"

"Bill!" I hissed. "Why the hell didn't you tell me Mr. Moore needed a glyph of protection cast on him?"

"Lexie?" said Bill. "What's going on? Are you talking about your nine A. M.?"

"Yes, I'm talking about my first client," I said. "I told you to give me jobs I could handle. Why in the world did you send me to a guy who needs me to cast a glyph on him?"

"Did Larry come out of the basement without me noticing?"

"How the hell should I know?"

"Then there's your answer. You're next in line, girl."

The water in the sink gurgled. I couldn't help but glance at the back of the door. "You're missing the point. What makes you think I'm capable of casting a glyph of protection?"

"I told you, don't sell yourself short. You crafted that potion last night, and you'd never done that before, either."

"You were helping! And we had a book with instructions on how to do it!"

"We might have a book on glyphs here at the house..."

"That doesn't help me right now, does it?"

Bill sighed. "What do you want me to tell you? You can always cancel on the guy."

"And lose our commission? You saw the mortgage notice, right?"

"I know it's a rhetorical question, but I'm the one who sent you on a job you're not completely qualified for, Lexie. What do you think?"

"What am I supposed to do, Bill?"

"In the long term? Learn how to cast the spell he asked you to. In the short term? Stall for time, maybe?"

"Wow. Thanks a lot. I'd never have come up with that myself."

"Well, what else do you want me to—"

I ended the call and hung my head as I leaned over the sink. At some point, I'd need to stop hanging up on my friends and family after getting into arguments with them, but it wasn't as if anyone was making it easy on me. All I wanted was for the Nyte Patrol to work, and yet Larry and Tank refused to help, Bill and Dawn weren't helping enough, and my family seemed to think I was wasting my time on a useless endeavor that wasn't going anywhere. Maybe they were right. *Shit!*

I took another deep breath and stuffed my phone back into my pocket. I could do this. I'd spent all my life working on a team. Some of that was spent carrying folks who weren't pulling their weight.

I turned the water off and headed back into the living room. Gary looked up from the couch expectantly. "There you are."

"Yes," I said. "I'm ready to begin now. We can leave the furniture where it is for the time being, but I'll need your flak jacket."

Mr. Moore looked at me and blinked. "I'm sorry, my *what?*"

"Flak jacket," I said. "Tactical vest. Bulletproof vest. They're all the same thing. I'll need that before we can begin."

Gary spread his hands. "But... I don't have a bulletproof vest."

"You don't?" I feigned surprise. "If you don't have one, then what am I supposed to cast the glyph on?"

Gary's eyes narrowed, and he seemed to be doubting himself. "I thought you'd cast it on me. I'm the one in need of protection."

I shook my head in a slightly condescending manner. "Mr. Moore, I'm sorry, but unfortunately it doesn't work that way. I can't enchant people, only objects."

"Well, what about something else? I have plenty of things I'm taking with me to Brazil."

I held up a hand. "While I *could* cast a glyph on your cell phone or a ring, I wouldn't feel comfortable ensuring your safety that way. For the glyph to take maximum effect, it has to be cast on an object of protection to begin with. That's why I feel the flak jacket is the right choice—that and the roving gangs you mentioned. It'll help even when magic doesn't."

Gary stood. "But my flight is leaving at three thirty. How am I supposed to get a bulletproof jacket by then?"

I shrugged apologetically. "I'm sorry, Mr. Moore, but client safety is too important for me to send you into a danger zone with a glyph I'm not fully confident in. Perhaps you should push back your flight a few days."

Gary snapped his fingers, a look of determination crossing his face. "I'm going to need your cell phone number. I know a few guys. I'm going to see what I can do. If I can leave the house no later than one thirty... Are you going to be in the area all day?"

I forced myself to smile, wondering what I'd gotten myself into. "Of course. There might be a rush fee involved, but I'll do my best. Now if you're ready to take that number..."

12

I parked in the Brazos garage south of Jester dormitories on the UT campus and hiked the tenth of a mile to the Perry-Castañeda Library. PCL, as it was better known, was a monstrously ugly five story structure of flat grey concrete that housed the lion's share of the university's ten million plus scientific and literary volumes. Thanks to numerous late night cram sessions spent deep within the academic bunker, I knew the building like the back of my hand. I could probably find the engineering stacks blindfolded, and I knew which corners tended to be the quietest and most likely to be unoccupied during finals week.

That knowledge might eventually help me, but not before I tracked down who I was looking for. I headed through the automatic doors at the front of the library, past the checkout desk, and stopped at the elevators. I punched the call button and checked my phone as I waited. It was already half past ten. Time was not on my side.

The door dinged and I hustled inside, hitting the button for the sixth floor. When the elevator stopped moving, I got out and headed toward the help desk. I had a few places I knew to look in case my first choice resulted in failure, but apparently I wouldn't need a plan B. A rather ridiculous looking individual stood beside a movable cart packed with books, a guy with frizzy hair, black-rimmed glasses, and several golden chains of different weights and lengths around his neck. He wore a paper-thin AC/DC T-shirt from the Let There Be Rock tour of 1977, and his faintly flared bell-bottom jeans looked like they might've been sourced from the same era.

His nose was stuck deep into a book titled *The Fourth Element* by someone I'd never heard of, E. Ellen Gracely. The cover looked pretty sweet though, with spectral blue flames dancing around a sexy young woman who looked equal parts human and robot.

"Hey, Adric."

The guy jumped, the book flying out of his hand. He bobbled it comically a few times before grabbing it by the cover and stuffing it behind his back. The look on his face shifted from one of guilt to suspicion as he focused on me. "Lexie? What are you doing here?"

I'd met Adric Wallow a few months ago during my first mission with the Nyte Patrol. He was a special type of magic user known as a bibliomancer, which meant he could reach into books and pull objects straight out of them. He'd pretty much given me a heart attack when he'd pulled a first edition iMac from the pages of a MacWorld magazine, mostly because it was the first act of magic I'd witnessed in person that I couldn't explain by other logical reasons. In the days that followed, I saw him do way weirder stuff, but at that point I'd already been attacked by a mob of naked vampires and travelled to a parallel universe mind prison with Larry, so his repeat efforts didn't have the same effect the first had.

I nodded toward the book. "Is that any good?"

He shrugged. "It's not bad. It scratches a certain itch."

"What itch is that? The itch for android erotica?"

Adric flushed. "This isn't smut. It's legitimate science fiction. The author was recently nominated for a Nebula Award for one of her pieces of short fiction."

"Short fiction can be erotica, too. It's probably easier to write than whole books. You just skip straight to the good stuff."

Adric frowned. "What do you want?"

"In a nutshell? I need your help."

Adric waggled the book at me. "Nuh-uh. I'm not getting suckered into this again. The last time you and your friends showed up, I got abducted by a vampire kingpin with a magic sword and nearly witnessed him transform a million bats into a vampire super army that would've wiped out life on Earth as we know it."

"*Nearly* being the operative word. And we saved you from him, remember?"

"That's like saying you saved me from being eaten by a crocodile after throwing me into a pit of hungry crocodiles. You're the reason I was in that mess in the first place."

"Come on, Adric," I said. "You're acting as if Romanov's actions were our fault. Besides, I'm not here to ask for your help beating off a supernatural mob boss."

"Nope. Sorry. Too busy." Adric tossed his book onto the cart and pushed it toward the exit. "Wish I could help, but I can't."

I moved into the way of the cart. "Will you stop it? You're clearly not too busy to help otherwise you would've been shelving books instead of reading them."

Adric scowled at me. "You need to get out of my way. You're committing numerous library workplace violations by prohibiting me from doing my job."

I frowned back. "Those aren't things. Besides, if you don't help me, I'll tell your employers you were slacking off at work."

Adric scoffed. "You think they don't know I read on the job? This is a *library*."

"I'll tell them you're living in an abandoned janitor's closet and that you've been stealing food from the community fridge."

Adric pulled himself up. "I've never stolen anyone's lunch in my life. I buy all my own canned foods and granola bars!"

I didn't move out of the way. "I'm not asking you to do anything crazy. I just need a crash course in magic. You of all people should be able to give me some pointers."

Adric's displeasure melted away, replaced with confusion. "You need training? Don't you live with a wizard?"

I rolled my eyes. "We're not on the best of terms."

Adric lifted an eyebrow. "You know, I heard rumors after that last case of yours, with the demon ghost. Is that—"

"I don't want to talk about it, okay?" My exclamation echoed off the walls, and I looked over my shoulder to make sure no one was staring at me angrily over their philosophy texts. I lowered my voice. "Can you help me or not?"

Adric leaned against his cart. "Are you trying to learn bibliomancy?"

"No. Regular magic. Spells, potions, enchantments. Glyphs, specifically."

Adric tipped his head. "Lexie, I'm not that type of magic user. I couldn't teach you to enchant a fly, just as Larry probably couldn't teach you the first thing about bibliomancy."

I sagged. "You went to magic school, didn't you? You must've picked up something. I'm drowning here. I need help."

Adric sighed. "Look. I don't know what's going on with you or Larry or anyone else in your circle of trust. I'm pretty sure I'm not the person you should've come to, but... as a librarian, it *is* my sworn duty to help you learn."

I peered at him quizzically. Was he being serious?

He continued. "And to be fair, although *I* may not be able to teach you what you want to learn, I *do* know a lot about books. Books are my thing, and there just so happens to be an archive on magic and the supernatural here. Whatever you're looking for, I'm sure we can find a book with the answer in it."

I shook my head. "That's not going to help. Larry has tons of books on magic, too, but they're all in Latin or Greek or Aramaic."

Adric lifted a finger. "Ahh. But we have translations here! That's right. Books in English. Come with me. I'll show you."

Adric squeezed past me and headed toward the elevators. I followed him and took a spot beside him as the doors opened in front of us. Adric pulled a key from his pocket, inserted it into the elevator panel, and turned it before pushing the button for the second sub-basement.

I gave him a nod as the elevator lurched into motion. "Does every UT library have a collection of magical tomes in the basement?"

"Well, the librarians aren't going to store them on the regular levels where anyone can check them out, would they?"

Adric genuinely seemed to miss my point. When the elevator stopped and we piled out, Adric led me through a set of narrow aisles packed tight with books ranging in age from yellowed to vellum. After a few twists and turns, he used another key to open a cage that was even more full of books than the aisles.

"Let's see." Adric ran his fingers across the stacks. "There should be some good introductory texts here. What did you say you needed help with? Wards?"

The air smelled of paper processing chemicals and glue. There must've been an area nearby for book repair. "Glyphs, of protection in particular."

"Alright. Let's try... *Elements of Defense*. That's a multi-volume series, but the first is probably all you need for now." Adric pulled a hefty book from the rack and handed it to me. *"Wards, Glyphs, and Runes.* Need that one. Oh, *Basics of Enchantment in the Mortal Realm.* That one's probably better. And *Theory of Portal Magic?* That might be more advanced than you need, but it couldn't hurt. Take it anyway. That'll get you started on the stuff you're most interested in. Tomorrow you can come back and we can swap them out for books on other disciplines."

My arms already ached from the weight of the tomes. *"Tomorrow?"*

Adric looked at me, realization settling in. "Right. You're probably not much of a speed reader. It's hard for me to remember how long it takes non-bibliomancers to absorb knowledge."

I glanced at my arms. Thousands of pages. Tens of pounds. Unknown numbers of ten syllable words I'd never heard before because they didn't exist in the average person's lexicon, and I had maybe three hours to get a working knowledge of the basics?

I smiled, trying to force some hope through me. "I don't suppose any of these come in audio?"

13

My stomach rumbled as I drove past Juan in a Million, Austin's famous breakfast taco institution on East Cesar Chavez. I would've pulled over and dived headfirst into a steaming plate of *migas* if not for the fact that it was after sundown and the place closed at three—that and the fact that I was running late for my next appointment.

I glanced at my console, hoping to catch a glimpse of an energy bar or a pack of trail mix, anything to quell the gnawing sensation occupying my empty belly. I even would've settled for cold fries, but all I spotted was the Red Bull I'd cracked before leaving my last job. I plucked it and drained the last few drops at the bottom of the can, puckering as the now warm liquid hit my tongue. The teal and red storefront of Diablo Piercing and Tattoo passed me by as I plopped the can back into the cupholder. I glanced at my phone, scared I'd missed the turn off, only to see it was the next street.

I pumped the brakes, tires screeching as I turned onto a small residential street. I glanced at my phone, angry it hadn't warned me with impending directions. The maps app was still open as I activated the thing with my thumb, but the sound had been muted. I cursed, wondering which of the elder gods I'd angered to make my day such a disaster—although, to be fair, it could've gone worse.

I'd spent most of the morning cramming from the books Adric loaded into my arms only to rush off at half past noon to attend a client meeting with a couple who wanted me to craft a fertility potion for them. Apparently, they didn't believe in things like "science" and "modern medicine" and preferred to take a more medieval approach to their baby-making. Before I'd had a chance to lie my way through assurances about the ultimate efficacy of the potion I'd make for them, Gary the witch-broker had called as he raced home after obtaining a bulletproof vest through what sounded like less than legal channels. I'd met him at his house, and even though I wasn't entirely sure what I was doing, I channeled the spark of magic that flowed through me and cast *something* upon the vest. The resulting ward fluctuated and pulsed in my mind's eye, smelling like a cross between a recently-fired gun and a cinderblock, but when Gary slipped it on, he claimed he felt fit as a fiddle. I really hoped it worked as the literature suggested. Beyond professional pride, I didn't know what I'd do if a protection ward I'd cast failed and I later learned Gary died due to my incompetence. Of course, I hadn't had much time to dwell on it as I'd received yet another call from Bill on my way out of his house.

So it was that I found myself pulling up in front of a quirky Austin bungalow at the foot of the Colorado River. The sun had dipped below the horizon, but there was still enough light left in the sky to illuminate the odd menagerie that occupied the home's front lawn. Pink flamingoes stood alongside cement frogs. Porcelain garden gnomes surrounded a gurgling stone

fountain, one with a weeping cherry hanging over it. A roughly
life-sized lion sculpture made entirely of rusted sheet metal
lazed beside the stepping stone path to the miniature home's
front porch, which itself featured a couple wicker chairs and an
excessive number of wind chimes.

I stuffed my phone into my pocket, shook my head and
blinked a few times to banish the exhaustion that was creeping
in on me, and headed out of the 'burban. Gravel crunched
underfoot, and wood creaked as I ascended the porch steps. A
screen door covered a painted red wooden one behind it, and a
sign to the right mounted upon the siding read "Miriam's
Mystical Healing. Please use knocker."

At least I knew I was in the right place. I opened the screen
door and slammed the bronze knocker down a few times. True
to form, the thing was shaped like a goat's head.

A few seconds later, I heard the wooden floor underneath
my feet creak again, and the door pulled back. A woman stood
in the gap, five foot nothing if even that, with skin a few shades
darker than mine and black hair tinged with the occasional
strand of gray tied into a long braid. She didn't have a single
visible wrinkle upon her brow or around her eyes, but eyes like
wet obsidian told a different story about her age.

She smiled at me, her teeth bright and white. "Ah. You must
be Lexie."

I'd seen dark eyes before—my own were a deep russet in
color—but I could barely even distinguish her pupil from her
iris. I tried not to stare. "That's right. How did you know?"

"Bill told me over the phone you'd be coming. Besides, it's
after hours." The woman pointed to the sign at my right.
Indeed, the hours of business were listed, and she'd closed up
shop long ago.

"I'm Miriam, by the way," she said. "Please, come in. We're letting all the cold air out."

She didn't have to ask me twice. Despite the short trek from my truck to the house, I could already feel beads of sweat forming under my blouse. I hustled inside as Miriam closed the door behind me. On first glance, the interior of the home was as unorthodox as the garden. Half the walls were covered with murals of animals and landscapes, while others were covered with mosaics made of colored glass and bits of glazed porcelain. The furniture was an eclectic mixture of distressed wood, tarnished bronze, and spindly metal things that had been painted the color of Fiestaware.

Miriam didn't bother locking the door. Her straw-colored sun dress swayed around her ankles as she came to a stop. She looked me up and down in a fraction of a second, still smiling, but in a reserved, perfunctory manner. "I take it Larry wasn't available."

Was that a subtle dig? "Unfortunately not. He's on a... sabbatical, I guess you could say."

"Oh." Miriam's eyebrows rose. "He's away on travel? Last I'd heard he was in town."

"No. He's around."

"Focused on his studies, then?"

"On certain ones, yeah. How do you know him?"

Miriam tipped her head. "We've worked together. He's aided me on castings a time or two. The tricky ones I wasn't sure how to handle. As proud as I am of being self-taught, there are occasional situations where a classical magic education could help me."

I perked up. "So you're a witch?"

"Witch doctor, to be precise." She waved toward the front of the house. "I'm sure you saw the sign. Miriam's Mystical Healing. I mean it in the legitimate sense, not the kind traveling quacks use." Miriam ushered me toward a sitting room with what looked like patio furniture in it, despite it being inside. "So you're Larry's protege?"

"I'd say apprentice. I'm still learning."

"Aren't we all?" Miriam's smile seemed to have lost the suspicion that first lingered in it. "Learning is a life-long process. There's always something we don't understand, and the more we know, the more we're aware of the gaps in our knowledge. The good news is you have a mentor. Larry always struck me as quite competent, professionally speaking, which means you must've shown promise for him to take you under his wing."

The praise left me feeling hollow. Everything Miriam had said was true enough—Larry's own spell picked me to head the Nyte Patrol, after all—but Larry hadn't spent much time training me in the use of magic, and I certainly didn't feel like I knew what I was doing. I questioned myself every day. "Thanks. It's been a good experience so far, for the most part. I like the work."

Miriam took a seat. "Speaking of which, let's talk business. I'm assuming Bill sent you over because you have experience with summonings?"

I lowered myself into the wicker chair opposite Miriam. "I guess that depends. What sort of summonings are we talking about?"

Miriam lifted an eyebrow. "Not the demonic kind, I assure you. I have a client who's suffering from a fairy pox. *Vesicarum capra pustulis correptus.* The festering goat pox. A nasty ailment, if I'm being honest. I've tried to cure the poor soul with the usual tonics and tinctures, but the pox refuses to subside.

Personally, I think there's something else going on, so I've decided to summon the fairy who gave my client the pox to ask it some questions and see if there's more to this particular strain than meets the eye."

"How do you know who gave him the pox in the first place?"

"I don't," said Miriam. "But I lanced one of my client's pustules and turned the liquid into a magical lure. If we place it at the core of the summoning circle and cast the proper spells around it, the fairy responsible for the pox should appear."

Normally, the thought of pus and pustules would've made me gag, but I was too nervous about the task before me to waste energy being disgusted. "Miriam, I have to be honest. I've done summoning work before, but I've never done anything with a magical lure. I wouldn't even know where to start..."

"Oh. Well, I don't need you for that," said Miriam. "I can handle the summoning myself. What I can't do is summon the little brat who cursed my client and maintain quality defensive measures around the circle while I interrogate the bugger. Fairies are notoriously tricksy. It wouldn't surprise me in the least if I brought it here only for it to try and escape and curse me with an even worse pox on its way out."

A flicker of hope appeared. "So... you need a ward."

"Precisely." Miriam looked at me expectantly. "You're up to the task?"

I swallowed back a lump of doubt. At least I'd already studied and practiced. "Let's do it."

14

I STOOD IN MIRIAM'S BACKYARD, WHICH THANKS TO A similar decorative aesthetic and the lack of a fence felt surprisingly similar to her front yard. Moonlight filtered down on me from between wisps of passing clouds, but there was plenty of light from manmade sources as well. Before starting her work, Miriam had lit about three dozen candles scattered among the garden gnomes and pink flamingos. After making her way through the garden with a grill lighter, Miriam had stopped at a pair of metal balls that hung from chains, one from the edge of her back porch, another from the low hanging branch of a persimmon tree. With each, she'd pulled out a cylindrical metal section from the top and held the lighter among the holes on the sides, waiting until a sweet smelling smoke began to pour from the contraption before putting the cylinder back in the ball. Miriam had referred to them as thuribles, although I was pretty sure the term only applied to ones used in religious ceremonies. Then again, what else would she call them? Hanging metal incense pots?

With the light of the candles flickering over us and the

wind carrying the incense's smoky, perfumed scent through the air, Miriam had crossed to her fire pit and begun lighting another two dozen candles that surrounded it. Although bits of spent coals and soot littered the bottom of the pit, the meticulous nature of the stones laid around the edge made it clear this was the magic circle Miriam used for spell castings. It was smart. Why draw a new circle each time when you could have a permanent one installed, one that served double duty for warming your face in the winter and making s'mores to boot?

I waited patiently while Miriam dealt with the candles. My first lesson from Larry had been on magic circles. He'd instilled in me that the only necessary elements of a circle were the establishment of the exterior by a magic user and the circle's physical location. Apparently, there were magical wells that could impact the efficacy of circles nearby, not to mention plants that contained latent magical energies, such as Rowan trees, and places that gained magical energy due to events that transpired there, such as graveyards. According to Larry, the addition of incense and candles didn't do a darn thing to increase a circle's power. Then again, if the ritual of lighting them put Miriam into the proper mental state to perform her magic, that alone made them worthwhile. Plus it gave me time to revisit my studies from earlier in the day and prepare myself for what would be asked of me.

As a flame bloomed from the last candle's wick, Miriam straightened, deposited the lighter upon a nearby steel mesh table, and returned to the edge of the circle. She gave me a nod. "I'm ready to begin. Are you?"

"I think so. But be sure to walk me through your expectations as we go. I've found that communication is key to success when it comes to magic." And sports, and really any team activity. At least I had experience with those.

"Of course." Miriam waved her hand at the stone circle, and I felt a pulse of power leap from the ground. "I'll activate the circle first. Prepare it for the spell. Once I have it primed, I'll have you cast the ward. Once you've assured me it's sound, I'll finish the summoning. Does that work?"

I hope it will, I thought. Instead of saying that, I merely nodded.

Miriam pulled a vial from the pocket of her dress. She leaned over the edge of the stones, pulled the stopper from the end, and upended the contents upon the dirt. The candlelight didn't give me the best view, but whatever liquid had been in there quickly absorbed into the soil. All for the best, I supposed. I certainly didn't want to contract any goat pox from the serum.

Miriam put the vial back into her pocket. She closed her eyes and begun speaking in a low voice. I'd half expected Latin, but instead she spoke in a language that was completely foreign to me, with lots of p's and k's and tz and ch sounds. It was heavy on consonants with what to me seemed short, choppy word segments. One snippet sounded like "hip yak crack."

My brow furrowed as she spoke, but I felt a rush of power leap up from the carefully placed stones. The circle glowed with a magenta aura in my mind's eye, smelling like a mix of mint, freshly tilled earth, and sulfur. I wrinkled my nose, but there was nothing there. The Smell was purely magical.

Miriam quieted, and her eyes opened. She nodded at me.

"That wasn't any of the ancient languages I've heard before," I said. "Is it a Native American tongue?"

"It's Mayan," she said. "Sometimes referred to as Ch'olan. The modern variant, or at least the one I learned, is known as

K'iche. It's very common in the Guatemalan highlands where I grew up."

That explained Miriam's unique look. I'd pinned her as Central American when I first saw her, but I had no idea of her nationality.

She extended a hand. "I've primed the circle. I pass it to you."

I nodded. This time, it was my turn to close my eyes. As I did so, I focused on the energies pulsing in front of me. I may not have been an expert on manipulating magical energies yet, but one of the few things I'd improved upon in leaps and bounds over the last couple weeks was feeling the magic around me. I sensed it now, beating with its own life force, a crude shell emerging from the ring of stones to shimmer in space over it. The potion I'd consumed the night before helped me key in on it, helped me isolate it, and beyond that, helped me spot the imperfections. Spots in the aura that were dull and smelled of nothing at all.

I hadn't expected Smell to help me cast spells, but perhaps I'd underestimated the power that an additional sense could provide. Like a blind man feeling his way by touch, I reached out, using the scent of the magic circle to suss out the weak spots. I grabbed ahold of the swirling energies, casting simple wards that I'd learned from Adric's books earlier in the day. Without moving, I reached out and swiveled around the circle, checking it from all sides. After patching a half-dozen spots, the shell's aura changed to a slightly lighter shade of magenta, and the sulfurous Smell I'd picked up on faded, leaving only those of mint and soil.

Just to be on the safe side, I gathered all the energy left available to me and cast the biggest ward I could, one that descended over the circle like a parachute and melted into the grass at my feet. Only when I could feel its strength alongside the smaller patches I'd cast did I open my eyes.

"Alright," I said. "I think we're good."

Miriam looked at the circle, a deep dive that suggested she was using more than her eyes. "Excellent. Time to find out what sort of pox we're up against."

Miriam extended a hand and spoke in Mayan again, though this time she didn't shut her eyes. She focused on the fire pit. The aura underneath my wards glowed and pulsed. Air rushed in toward the circle, bringing with it some of the smoke from the thuribles, and with an audible *pop*, a being appeared amidst the candles.

But it wasn't a fairy. It was the teensiest, tiniest mini horse I'd ever laid eyes on, roughly the size of a Corgi and twice as shaggy. The thing tilted its head, looking about in confusion.

I burst out in laughter before cutting myself off abruptly. I looked at Miriam, feeling sheepish. "Sorry. That was rude. I was expecting a fairy. I wasn't prepared for this."

The mini horse spun toward me, its fuzzy eyebrows dancing. "What the hell is that supposed to mean?"

I blinked, my face slackening in shock. "Wait... it can talk?"

"Of course it can talk," said Miriam. "Fairies are perfectly capable of speech."

"But... this isn't a fairy," I said. "I've met a fairy. He was human. I mean, at least he looked it, even if he was on the short side."

"Yeah, well, you look like shit, too, thank you very much." The mini horse snorted at me and tossed its head. "And for the record, I'm a he, not an it. How the hell would you like it if I mis-gendered you, bro?"

"Fairies can take multiple forms, especially in the fae realm," said Miriam. "This one apparently chose to resemble a dwarf mini horse, for some reason."

"The reason is that chicks dig it," he said. *"Especially* once they see what I'm packing down under. Want a taste?"

The mini horse reared and pawed at the edge of the magic circle. The wards I'd put in place sparked as his hooves bounced off them.

Miriam grimaced. "Settle down. No one wants to see that. Lexie, keep a hold on those wards. I trust this guy about as far as I could throw him."

"Eh. I'd fly farther than you think," said the horse. "But if you take a run at chucking me, be sure to cradle me properly. One hand under my chest, another between my back legs. That's where I'm the most ticklish, if you catch my drift."

I frowned. Although I'd prepared myself to deal with a pox-ridden sprite, I hadn't mentally braced for the possibility of coming face to face with a sexually-deviant talking mini horse. I tightened my hold on the wards and gave Miriam a nod. "We're good."

Miriam took a step toward the edge of the magic circle. "Listen up, Secretariat. In case you haven't noticed, you're in a bit of a predicament."

"First of all, lady, the name's Cash. Want to know why?"

"Not really."

"Cause I make it rain on them bitches, that's why!" Cash whinnied in mirth. "And second of all, I don't appreciate being summoned out of my peaceful abode right when I'm about to get my swerve on."

I suddenly had a terrible premonition. "Miriam? How did this client of yours contract the pox they're fighting?"

She shook her head. "Maybe not in the way he told me. I almost don't want to know. What matters now, *Cash,* is what exactly you did to my client and how I can cure them?"

Cash shook his head, his tiny mane flying. "Whoa, there. Back it up, toots. What are you talking about?"

"His name is Charles Vandersnoot. Goes by Chuck. You cursed him with a festering goat pox—or transferred it to him via some other means. I don't need to know how. What I need from you is how to cure it."

"Look, Lady. I don't know any Chuck, and I'm not into dudes, so it sounds like you summoned the wrong fairy. Now if you could send me back to my place so I can finish my *bow-chicka-wow-wow…*"

Miriam lifted a hand. "You weren't summoned by chance. I traced the strain of goat pox directly to you, and the summoning circle did the rest. Tell us what you know."

Cash's nostril's flared. "You realize what you're getting in the middle of, don't you? The attention of the fine filly in my bedroom will stray sooner rather than later, and I was almost worked up to a lather."

"Better get cracking, then. Tell us what you know."

"I'm telling you, I don't know anything about a pox. Now let me out of here and—"

Miriam whipped a hand toward the magic circle, and a bloom of purple color exploded upon the invisible hemisphere over the stones. A ripple that I felt in my muscles ran through the wards as she did so. "Enough! *Tell us what you know.*"

Cash's eyes widened. He pawed the ground with one hoof, and a low, inhuman growl whistled from between his equine teeth. Good thing I already had a grip on the wards because I didn't have time to react when his body blurred into action.

Visually, it looked like a special effect you'd see in a science fiction movie, where someone's body phased in and out through alternate dimensions. The event was totally different when experienced through my magical senses though. A tidal wave of energy slammed into the protective shell over the circle. My wards pulsed and hissed, and the pressure wave nearly knocked me off my feet. I stumbled backward, my arms flailing, but even as I struggled to keep my body from falling, I clamped hold of the wards and *squeezed*. I felt their heat on my face, saw their aura shift to a bright red color. They shook violently, but they didn't give.

The ordeal was over in a few seconds. Cash's blurry form coalesced back into that of a stunted mini horse, though he slumped and hung his head. Heavy snorts blew through his nostrils, his chest heaving with exertion. His voice was cowed when he spoke. *"Damn you..."*

Miriam shot me a sly smile before kneeling at the side of the fire pit. "Work with us. We're not asking a lot."

"But you're asking for something," huffed Cash. "Demanding, more like, and that's not how we roll. If you want something from a fairy, you have to make a trade. Everyone knows that."

I didn't. "Doesn't seem like you're in much of a position to strike a deal."

"It's about saving face," said Miriam. "But I'm willing to play along. So here's the deal. We'll agree to let you go, and in exchange you'll tell us about the pox. Fair?"

Cash's lips pulled back. "How is that fair? You're the ones who've imprisoned me!"

Miriam shrugged. "You wanted a trade. I've offered one. The sooner you accept, the sooner you can get back to your feisty filly."

Cash nickered. "Fine. I know Charles. He's a good-for-nothing picaroon, if you ask me. He backed out of a trade we agreed to, and in return, I cursed him with the pox. And no, it wasn't sexual, in case you're wondering. If he's your client, I hope you got payment in advance, because he's liable to stiff you the same as he did me."

"Noted," said Miriam. "How do I cure the pox?"

"What do you mean, how do you cure it?" asked Cash. "You're a witch doctor, aren't you? I can tell by the flavor of this circle. Are you really trying to tell me you can't cure a simple festering goat pox?"

"I can cure simple ones all day long," said Miriam, a frosty nip entering her voice. "The one you cast is anything but."

"I feel like I should take that as a compliment," said Cash, "but really, it wasn't. Are you using a traditional Bell's swamp root potion?"

"Yes," said Miriam.

"With eye of newt? Honest to goodness newt, not plain salamanders?"

"Of course."

"And root of the Nyssa genus?"

"Tupelos, yes."

"Freshly sourced?"

Miriam's eyebrow rose. "How fresh?"

"No more than three months old. It can lose potency after that."

"Huh." Miriam stood. "That must be it. I think I've had my batch for at least a year."

"Well, there you have it," said Cash. "Now could I *please* go back to my home?"

Miriam smiled. "Pleasure doing business with you, Cash. Try not to spread any more poxes out of spite."

She waved her hand, and with a similar pop to the one I'd heard the first time, the mini horse disappeared. The aura surrounding the magic circle faded, as did the Smell of mint and tilled soil, but I kept the wards in place regardless. Better safe than sorry.

Miriam noticed. She gestured with a couple fingers. "You can let those go now. He's gone—and I dare say he won't be testing the bonds of his prison if we ever have a reason to summon him again. Nicely done, by the way. I have to assume he gave you everything he had."

I released my grip on the wards, but they didn't immediately wink out of existence. Rather, they started to melt, like ice cream on a hot day. "Thanks. It's always nice when spells work the way they're supposed to." And I hadn't been totally sure they would. Successes in magic had been few and far between for me.

Miriam smiled. I don't think she could read my mind, but I wasn't totally sure of the extent of her powers. "I'll be able to take it from here, although if Cash was to be trusted, perhaps I should get an advance from Vandersnoot before I order more swamp roots. Thanks again for your help, Lexie. If I ever have need of someone to watch my back during a summoning, I'll know who to call—and who to ask for. No offense to Larry, of course."

I felt the corners of my lips creep up of their own accord. It felt good to be praised, especially when the praise was earned.

I turned to head back to the Suburban, thoughts of a Kerbey Lane Cafe dinner on my mind, but I paused. "Speaking of

Larry... you've been working as a witch doctor for a while, I presume?"

Miriam's brow lifted in curiosity. "Over a decade. Closer to two. Why?"

"I was wondering if you had time for a consult. There's something I could use your help with..."

15

I WOKE TO HANDS SHAKING ME VIOLENTLY, AS WELL AS AN agitated voice hissing my name. "Lexie. Lexie! Wake up!"

My eyes snapped open to see Dawn hovering over me, clad in a black tank top and with her hair looking surprisingly unkempt. Sunlight streamed through the window in my bedroom. A quick glance at my clock showed it was half past eight.

I struggled to gather my thoughts. "What... what's going on? Is everything okay?"

Dawn scoffed. "Is everything okay? *Is everything okay?* Do you think I'd be shaking you awake if everything was fine and dandy?"

I gathered more information in my groggy stupor. The house was still standing. It didn't appear to be on fire. I couldn't hear any screams. "What's the problem? Is someone hurt?"

Dawn stood and paced next to my bed. "The problem, *Lexie,* is that we're overworked. Understaffed. Bill called me eight times yesterday. *Eight times!* Want to guess how many of those calls involved new assignments? Take a wild guess."

I rubbed my eyes. "Eight?"

"Ding ding. We have a winner. And do you have a guess on how long it takes to meet eight new clients, hear their problems, question them, investigate their concerns, take their calls, travel between their homes and places of business, all without a car of your own?"

"Um..."

"I was working until four in the morning, Lexie. *Four.* Don't even ask when I got home, or what the stupid Uber driver insisted on talking to me about on the ride back here at four freaking forty-five."

Dawn paced rapidly and spoke even quicker. Her arm shook, and it was only then that I noticed the travel cup of coffee in her hands. "Is that your second cup?"

"Fourth," she said. "Maybe fifth. I don't remember. The point is, we can't do this on our own. Or to be more specific, *I* sure as hell can't do this myself. Not on two and a half hours of sleep. Not when Bill has already called to notify me of another job he's signed us up for, *tonight!"*

"Another one? Isn't it Saturday?" I glanced at my clock again, as if that would tell me the day of the week.

"You think that matters?" said Dawn. "When you run your own business, you work every day of the week, whenever the jobs arrive. You work for the client, when *they* want you to. Why are you still in bed?"

"What? Sorry." I tossed the sheets to the side and sat up, still feeling less than a hundred percent. "I thought you said this new job was tonight."

"Yeah, but it's not a simple one. We're supposed to provide security to a three hundred person gala for the Texas Memorial

Museum. Three hundred people, Lexie! How in the world are we supposed to do that? I'm going to kill Bill."

I avoided the obvious reference or pointing out the fact that he was already dead. Dawn didn't seem like she was in a mood to appreciate either. "Well… I'm not sure. But on first thought I'd say we'll probably need Larry and Tank's assistance."

Dawn whirled on me and stuck a finger in my direction. "Exactly. Except I've already thought of that. When I went to the basement to find Larry, he'd barricaded himself behind a wall of furniture, and when I gave up and tried to rouse Tank, I found he wasn't even in his room!"

I blinked. "Again?"

"What do you mean, again?"

"He was gone yesterday morning, too. Came home while you were out for your jog."

"Whatever," said Dawn. "The point is, he's not there. He's not around to help. No one is. It's just you and me. So tell me. How in the world are we supposed to get this done? Huh? Tell me. *How?*"

Heat crept into my cheeks in response to the ire directed my way, but I wrestled it down. It wasn't focused at me, even if I was the recipient. I knew because I'd felt the same way over the past couple days, even if a liter of coffee and three hours of sleep hadn't frazzled me the same way it had her.

I sighed. "We can't do it all, Dawn. I'm not arguing we can. I was trying to, sure, because I'm not the kind to take defeat lying down. I've always tried to work through problems, and when others don't help, I'm stubborn enough to think I can fix everything myself. But we can't keep the Nyte Patrol afloat on our own. We need to bring Larry and Tank back into the fold."

Dawn collapsed into my office chair, the nervous energy leaving her with a breathy sigh. "Well... I'm glad you see it."

"But it's not that easy," I said. "I've tried to talk to them, too. They don't want to let me in."

Dawn turned and looked out the window, her eyes distant. "I know what you mean. I can't get through to them. Christ, Lexie. I thought *we* were supposed to be the moody, emotional ones."

Somewhere downstairs a phone rang. "Yeah, well, women haven't been the ones to plunge the world into continent-spanning wars every few years for the last couple millennia, so I don't know how much faith to put into that particular gender stereotype."

Dawn shook her head before casting me a sorrowful glance. "So what do we do?"

I gave the question some thought. Really, I did. Ultimately, I found myself shrugging. "I don't know. I've tried talking to them, but it didn't get me anywhere, same as you. Maybe if we tackle them together. Have an intervention of sorts."

"Might work with Tank," said Dawn. "At least what he's going through, the death of a loved one, is a normal part of human existence. Larry's predicament, on the other hand..."

"Tell me about it."

Dawn's phone rang, and she gave an exasperated sigh. It wasn't until she pulled the phone from the pocket of her tight capris that her face twisted in anger, though. "Oh, for crying out loud." She stood and moved to the door jam. *"Bill, if you wanted to talk you could just call out!"*

Bill's voice echoed up the stairs. "It's not me, actually. I'm forwarding you a call through the phone system."

"Are you serious?" shouted Dawn. "Don't you know how

overworked we are? The least you can do is answer the phones! That's your one job."

"It's Frank Connors," called Bill. "Just answer it."

Dawn swore and swiped the phone. She brought it to her ear. "Hello?"

In a span of seconds, her eyes lost their ire. "Yeah. Okay. Sure. We'll be right there."

I stood as she tucked the phone into her pocket. "What's going on? Don't tell me Frank is looking to hire us, too." Police jobs tended to be interesting but far more involved than civilian fare.

"Not exactly," said Dawn. "He found Tank."

16

I'D CALLED AHEAD, SO FRANK MET US INSIDE THE DOORS TO
the station next to the help desk. He stood with his arms crossed
over his chest, the freshly sheared ends of his salt-and-pepper
hair sticking straight out to the sides and his thick mustache
bristling. He looked less than happy.

"There you are," he said. "I was about ready to leave a
deputy here for you instead."

I tilted my sunglasses onto the top of my head, trading the
outdoor sun for the cold sterile light of the police headquarters.
"I called as we were parking. It only took us a few minutes."

"Minutes I could've spent working. You realize my job
doesn't involve coddling you and your associates, right?"

Dawn wasn't the apologizing type. She gave Frank a firm
nod. "Where's Tank?"

"In the cells with the rest of the drunks. We'll take the elevator." Frank headed off through the seating area at the front of
the building, currently populated only by a few police officers, a
woman who looked like she was being booked for solicitation,
and a hispanic family that might've been waiting there for days

based on the heavy bags under their eyes. Phones rang behind a movable partition, and somewhere in the distance I heard a slurred voice yelling and another more confident voice telling the first to sit down and shut up.

Frank didn't speak as he walked, and he crossed his arms again once he'd pushed the button for the elevators. The scowl plastered across his face spoke to his mood, but I wasn't going to be cowed into silence by that alone. I needed answers.

"You didn't say much to Dawn over the phone," I said. "Mind telling us what happened?"

The elevators dinged and the doors opened. We piled in, and Frank punched the button for the basement. "Not much to tell. The boys picked him up last night on Sixth Street at quarter after five. By the racket he was making, you'd think he was in the middle of a bare knuckle brawl, but when our officers rolled up, they found him with his pants around his ankles, urinating on a fire hydrant and yelling something about Afghanistan."

"A fire hydrant?" I lowered my voice, even though we were alone in the elevator. "He wasn't in bear form, was he?"

Connors shook his head. "Thankfully not, but that doesn't mean he was in a mood to come quietly. My men and women in uniform had to call for backup, and that's simply because he was drunk and disorderly. Can you imagine if he'd wanted to do us harm? People could've gotten hurt. *My people.*"

The elevator doors slid open and spit us out. A wall of bars separated us from a cluster of holding cells beyond. A hum of fluorescent lights mixed with the low grumble of unhappy inmates. The scent of bleach mostly overpowered the lingering stink of vomit and alcohol.

"Where's Tank?" asked Dawn.

"Last cell on the right." Frank pointed. "We decided it would be better to keep him isolated from the others, given what we know he's capable of. Talk to the discharge officer at the desk. They're expecting you."

Dawn nodded and headed toward the officer in question, her back stiff and straight. She wasn't any happier than I was to be here.

I lingered behind with Connors. "Look, Frank. I'm sorry about Tank. He's been going through some things. You remember how he lost his ex-wife."

Frank ushered me toward the corner. He checked over his shoulder as he lowered his voice, making sure there was no one else nearby. "I'm going to be honest with you, Lexie. I like you guys. I've known Larry a long time, and he's done me a number of solids, but you need to hear me when I tell you this isn't a warning."

"I know. I'm sorry," I said. "We're going to talk to him. We're—"

Frank took a step toward me, looming over me. "That's not what I mean. Neither you nor I consider Tank a menace, but the totem pole rises above me. There are people on the top who don't have such a charitable opinion of him and his abilities. Tank is officially at the end of his rope. I had to pull as many strings as I could to keep him out of jail when he assaulted a police officer during the incident with the spirit who killed his ex-wife, and it was *only* because of the circumstances involved that I was able to cut him any slack. That goodwill has been spent. If he gets caught breaking the law one more time, even for jay walking, there are going to be consequences. The people who decide these things aren't going to slap him with a light sentence either, not knowing what he's capable of, and there's not a damn thing you or Larry is going to be able to do about it. Do you hear me?"

I nodded, a lump taking up the better part of my throat. "Loud and clear."

Frank turned as the door to the holding cells creaked. The discharge officer held the door while Dawn and Tank walked through, the former helping the latter. Like the last time I saw him, Tank was wearing sweats, but this time he'd lost his shirt. He stumbled as he walked, and his eyes were mostly closed. Good thing Dawn had an arm around him.

"Speaking of Larry," said Frank, "how is he?"

"He's been better," I said. "He's still not quite ready to face the world."

Frank looked at me, the anger in his eyes mostly replaced with concern. "Are you ever going to tell me what happened out on that farm?"

"Someday. Once Larry's ready to talk about it. It's not my story to tell." Dawn gave me a nod, and I turned toward the elevators. "Thanks again for the assist, Frank. We won't waste it."

17

Dawn reached a hand toward the radio of my Suburban, turning down the volume to Guns N' Roses' "Sweet Child o' Mine." She'd been the one to turn the volume up as we left the station. Even though I wasn't the best at reading expressions, there wasn't any doubt in my mind why she'd wanted to drown out the conversation. The muscles bulging from her jaw spoke volumes.

But rage never lasts, even when it's directed at the ones you care about. With each passing stoplight, Dawn's breath grew more regular, and it no longer looked like she was ready to crack walnuts with her teeth.

Dawn didn't turn in her seat, but she spoke clearly, her voice carrying over the guitars. "We need to talk, Tank."

I glanced in the rear-view mirror. Tank slumped in the seat behind me, one of the random engineering T-shirts I'd gotten at a recruiting fair stretched tight over his chest and one of my UT Softball caps pulled down over his face. I couldn't hear snoring, but I wasn't entirely sure he was awake, either.

"You can't keep doing this to yourself," said Dawn. "Going

out every night? Trying to drink away the pain? It's not going to help. It's not going to solve your problems, though it's well on its way to creating some new ones. It sure as hell isn't going to bring Kiara back."

Tank didn't say anything, though he did slump further into his seat, thereby suggesting he was, in fact, awake.

Dawn took a long, slow breath, and I could hear a ripple of irritation creeping into her voice. "Don't you have anything to say for yourself? There are all kinds of places you could start. Saying you're sorry for publicly exposing yourself and pissing on a fire hydrant would be one option, or perhaps thanking us for bailing you out."

Tank grunted, and he turned his head toward the window.

Dawn shook her head as I turned onto Guadalupe. She flicked a hand toward the upcoming stoplight. "Turn right."

Our house was on West 21st, but that was in the other direction. "Huh? Why?"

"Just do it, will you?"

I'd already started to change lanes, so I merged back onto my side and hooked a right. "Where are we going?"

"The Littlefield Fountain," said Dawn.

"Ok. I guess I can park in the Brazos garage." It was where I'd parked yesterday to get to PCL.

"Not the garage," said Dawn. "Pull up in front. On the sidewalk."

"What?" I was already starting to pass the fountain by. "I can't do that. I'll get a ticket."

"Damnit, girl." Dawn reached over and cranked on the wheel. I tried to fight her, but she got the drop on me. The truck's wheels screeched as we fishtailed into the left lane, and I had to lay on the brakes to keep us from flipping over.

The tires thumped as we jumped the curb, but I didn't hear them pop, nor did I hear the metallic crunch of an axle being bent the wrong direction. I stared at Dawn as we shuddered to a stop, my heart beating like a drum. "Christ almighty. *What the hell was that?*"

Dawn didn't listen to me. She'd already hopped out the door and was storming around to the other side. Tank seemed oblivious to what was going on, but Dawn forced him into the moment when she pulled open the door he was slumped against. He flailed as he fell out of the car. Dawn kept him from face-planting on the concrete. She grabbed him by the arm and spun him around, whipping him around the back of the car.

Tank sputtered, stumbling wildly under Dawn's onslaught. "What the...? Dawn? What are you—?"

I jumped out of the car in time to see Dawn plant her feet at the edge of the fountain, shift her weight, and toss Tank into the crystal clear water like a seasoned judoka.

Tank reared out of the fountain, resembling the cast bronze warhorses behind him as he sprayed water from his mouth. He'd lost my baseball cap and his shirt stuck to him like glue. "Dawn! *What the hell?*"

I reached the edge of the fountain as Dawn jumped in after him. She landed on her feet, dancing through the foot and a half of water only to plant a hard shove straight to Tank's chest. The big man's arms flailed as he toppled into the water a second time.

He surged up, his body coiled and ready for a shove. "Dawn! Seriously! What—?"

Dawn's arm blurred as she whipped an open palm against Tank's cheek. The meaty *thwap* rang out with as much force as one from a professional wrestling ring. Tank's head spun and his eyes widened, first with shock and then with anger. "Why you little..."

Dawn didn't give him a chance to finish his thought. Her other arm flew through the air, landing a direct blow to Tank's other cheek.

"Ow!" Tank held a hand to his face. "Stop it! That hurts!"

Dawn didn't listen. She bore down on him, slapping with one arm and then the other. Tank held his forearms up to fend off the blows, but Dawn landed at least one for every two she flung.

"Stop it, Dawn! Ow! Hey. Do you hear me? *Ow!* Damnit, Dawn, stop. Are you even listening to me? What's gotten into you? *Ow!* Hey. Stop it. *STOP IT!*"

Tank reached out and grabbed both of Dawn's arms simultaneously, her hands suspended in mid-air, ready for another slap. Even with Tank's dark skin, I could see his cheeks glowing red. I also noticed at least a half-dozen students with backpacks had stopped to gape at the spectacle.

Dawn leaned in close, breathing hard and half soaked herself. "So you *can* feel that."

Tank's nostrils flared, his eyes wide with anger. "Of course I can feel it. *What the HELL is wrong with you?*"

Dawn leaned in against Tank's iron grip. "Seems to me you wouldn't be able to feel it. Not after all the beers you've drunk. The shots upon shots of vodka and whiskey and tequila. Not after the drugs, the sleepless nights, and God knows what else you've done to yourself. I know I wouldn't feel anything. I wouldn't feel a *god-damned thing.*"

Tank's eyes narrowed, and his jaw tightened. "You think I don't feel anything? You think I'm not in pain? That's why I've been drinking myself numb, why I've been shutting everyone out. Because I hurt. I'm in *agony*." Tank threw one of Dawn's arms to the wind and slammed his palm against his chest. "In here. It never stops. The pain rips me apart, every minute of every day. You have no idea what I'm feeling. What unending torture tears through me with every passing second. So you're damned right I feel it. It hurts. It *always* hurts."

Dawn's voice lowered, so that I had a hard time hearing it over the crash of water spraying from the back of the fountain. "So what you're saying is, the drugs and the alcohol and shutting yourself in—it doesn't work, does it?"

Something passed across Tank's eyes. "No."

Dawn leaned in further, but she didn't raise her free hand to strike him. "Then why do you keep doing it?"

Tank hung his head, but he didn't say anything.

"You lost her, Tank," said Dawn. "You'd already lost her once, but this time she's gone for good. You need to accept it."

Tank lifted his head. He was soaked, but his eyes glimmered with tears rather than spray. "I never accepted losing her the first time. How in the world am I supposed to accept it now?"

"By acknowledging your feelings. Facing them. Addressing them," said Dawn. "We can help you with it, but you need to help us, too. In case you haven't noticed, we're falling apart at the seams. We need you at our side, solving cases with us. Hell, we've got a security detail tonight and *we need you*."

Tank blinked. "What are you talking about?"

Dawn shook her head. "Christ. You really *haven't* noticed, have you?"

The crowd of student had grown, despite the fact that Dawn wasn't mercilessly slapping Tank anymore. Some of them were on their phones, the majority probably telling their friends about the crazies in the Littlefield Fountain, but some might've been calling the police. Given the warning we'd gotten from Detective Connors...

"Guys." I nodded toward the crowd. "You should probably get out of the fountain."

Dawn looked over Tank's shoulder and nodded. "Yeah. Come on. We'll fill you in as we go."

18

I pulled the Suburban to the back edge of the Nine Moons strip mall, right in front of the slope that led to the sewer main and the retention pond. I put the truck in park and killed the engine. Only then did Tank speak.

"I owe you an apology."

He sat in the passenger seat, wearing a pair of jeans and a plain gray shirt. He'd taken a shower after we'd gotten home, though there were still bags under his eyes. Chances are he should've stayed and taken a nap to be refreshed for our job later in the evening, same as Dawn had chosen to do, but after we'd filled him in on our state of affairs, he'd insisted on accompanying me to the woods to take a look at the prints I'd found. He'd done some tracking during his days in the marines. He hadn't said much of anything since he climbed into my truck, though.

I turned to face him. "Yeah. I suppose you do."

He looked me in the face. I could tell the aftereffects of the alcohol were still making his life hell, but he was making an effort. "I shut you out. I ignored you, and I wasn't willing to take the hand you offered when I was down. I don't know why I thought I could run away from my problems, but I did, and in doing so, I wasn't around to help when you needed me. I'm sorry for that. For all of it."

I reached out and grasped Tank by the shoulder. "Apology accepted. It's hard to be a good friend when you're going through hell."

Tank shrugged. "It's not an excuse."

"No, but it is an explanation." I nodded toward the woods. "You sure you want to do this now? We could just grab a cup of coffee and talk."

"I appreciate the offer, but part of me making good on my shitty behavior involves helping clear the backlog of work you and Dawn have been covering for me. Besides, I'm kind of curious about these tracks you found."

Tank cracked his door, and I did the same. I led the way down the embankment, past the drainage field, and into the trees. Pretty much at once, I realized I didn't know where I was going. When I'd dropped by two nights ago, everything had been dark, but I'd also been guided by a supercharged sense of Smell. I hadn't lost the sense entirely. If I focused, I could see faint auras lingering among the brush, and I think I detected a whiff of the lemony herb that had been among Augusta's mangled plants if not the scent of licorice I'd pulled from the dirt.

I took a few steps into the leaves, looking about as I tried to find the same markers I'd spotted the first time. There had been a patch of marshy earth. That's where I'd found the footprint. Had it been to the right, past the juniper with the low hanging branches? Maybe past the two jagged limestone boulders half-covered with pale green lichens?

I heard a snort behind me. "You don't remember where it is, do you?"

I sighed. "It was dark. I was using magic to guide me more than anything else."

Tank cracked a smile. I hadn't seen one of those in weeks. "Well, have at it. Don't let me hold you back, Sabrina."

"Pardon?"

"The teenage witch?"

I suppressed a groan. "I'm a couple months shy of being able to legally buy booze, meathead. But more on point, I was using a scent spell. Unfortunately, it's faded a bit since I was here last."

"As have the scents in question, I'm sure," said Tank. "That's okay. We can use traditional techniques to find what we're looking for. Any idea where you went?"

I gestured between the trees. "Straight-ish."

Tank rolled his eyes. "I see. No wonder you needed my help. Follow me, and tell me if you Smell anything."

Tank headed into the thickest of the underbrush, his eyes trained on the ground. He walked slowly, his head on a swivel as he glanced at the carpet of leaves on the forest floor, at the bases of trees where animals might've brushed up, and into the shadows under fallen logs. I stayed quiet, in part not to disturb him but also to focus on my magical senses. As I walked into the woods, I picked up more auras. There was a plant here, another there. The same sorts of herbs I'd noticed the first night. I even picked up on a strange fluttering aura near the tip of a cypress tree, but my eyes didn't reveal so much as a bird's nest among the high branches. On the one hand, it buoyed me that I was able to pick out Smells even after the effects of the potion should've worn off, but the fact that I couldn't detect the telltale scent of licorice nonetheless disappointed me.

"Hold on," said Tank. "I think I've found something."

He pushed a low-hanging branch out of the way and ducked underneath it. I joined him as he brushed a few leaves out of the way. "See?"

I looked at what he'd uncovered. In a patch of damp soil, there was a paw print of sorts, maybe a third the size of a human hand with stubby digits. Tank looked at me. "Was this it?"

I shook my head. "I found a footprint, much more human-like than that and big. Big enough to freak me out. That's why I wanted you to tag along."

"Not for my tracking skills, I see." Tank peered at the print closer. "It's weird. I don't think I've ever seen anything quite like this. It's not a raccoon, that's for sure."

I leaned in closer, too. I closed my eyes and focused with my powers. I sniffed, breathing deep of the magics. I couldn't detect any aura around the print, but...

Suddenly I smelled it. A hint of licorice.

My eyes snapped open. "This is it. It has the same Smell I picked up from Nine Moons. But... that doesn't make any sense."

"Why not?" asked Tank.

"Because the other track that most definitely did not come from the same being as this had the same Smell," I said. "Or at least I think it did. I was a little overwhelmed that night."

Tank brushed away more of the leaves. "Here's another one. A partial one anyway. Looks like the creature was headed toward the parking lot."

"Can you track it further?"

"I can try."

Tank hunched down, shuffling along the path we'd already taken. He brushed at the ground every so often, his eyes narrowing in thought. We made it halfway to the concrete expanse before he straightened. "I think I've lost it."

I glanced along our path. "But it was headed this way."

"Without a doubt."

I extrapolated the trajectory, which led out of the woods towards Nine Moons. "Any idea how old the tracks are?"

"Hard to say," said Tank. "I'd guess less than a day, but who knows?"

My brow furrowed. "I think we should have another chat with Ms. Shade."

I headed out of the woods. As I climbed the shallow slope and reached my car, I paused, staring at the back entrance of Nine Moons. "Hey. The crates are gone."

Tank paused beside me. "What crates?"

"These big black boxes. BSI left them. You know. Brute Squad Incorporated? Augusta called them to investigate the case, too."

"And they left a bunch of crates behind the store?"

"Yeah." I nodded toward the truck. "Come on."

I hopped inside and pulled the car around, parking in front of Nine Moons. The door chimes rang as I pushed my way inside. This time, Augusta was working the counter.

She wore a pleated chiffon gown with long sleeves that were big enough to smuggle watermelons in, though her hair had been tamed by the same headband as before. She grimaced when she saw me. "Oh. Right... It was Lexie, wasn't it?"

"Yeah, with the Nyte Patrol," I said. "This is one of our other associates, Tank Johnson. Do you have a minute?"

Augusta held up a hand. "I'm so sorry. I really should've called, but it slipped my mind. The case got solved."

I blinked. "What?"

At least Augusta had the decency to look sheepish. "It was BSI. I can't remember if I told you or not, but I called them when I didn't get an immediate response from you guys. They set up traps in back. Apparently, they dropped by last night to check them, and they'd caught the intruder who broke into my shop."

"They did?" I glanced at Tank, who stood there looking more confused than I was. "Who was it?"

"More like what was it," said Augusta. "A duende. Otis called this morning to tell me."

"Back up," I said. "A what?"

"Duende." Augusta brushed a stray lock of hair behind her ear. "They're tricky little spirits known for whistling and luring lost children into the woods, which I think was more of a problem hundreds of years ago than it is today. I thought they lived in Latin America, but perhaps climate change is pushing them further north. I'm speculating though. I don't know for sure."

"And they caught this thing behind your store?" said Tank.

"That's what Otis told me," said Augusta. "They managed to lure it inside with toenail clippings. Don't ask, because I couldn't tell you. They think it managed to get in the first time through the air conditioning system."

"Didn't you say you checked that?" I asked.

Augusta shrugged. "I must've missed it, I guess. Look, I apologize for not calling. I should've notified you they'd closed the case. It's my mistake."

My heart sank. I wasn't sure how much money we would've made from the job, but given our situation, every paycheck would help. "It's alright. Have a nice day, Ms. Shade."

Tank held the door for me as we headed back outside. His

passenger door clanged as he settled into his seat. "Well, that sucked."

The Suburban roared to life as I turned the keys in the ignition. "Yup. At least we have that security detail tonight. I hope they pay well."

19

SINCE BILL TOLD DAWN WE WERE PROVIDING SECURITY
for a Texas Memorial Museum gala, I'd figured the gala would
be held *at* the museum. That's why I was so surprised when my
phone guided me to a country club hidden in the hills of west
Austin.

The place was about as swanky as Austin got. A sprawling
building with hand cut limestone walls and a gleaming copper
roof sat behind a brick driveway circle. An overhang large
enough to cover a half dozen jumbo SUVs jutted over the front
doors, held up by columns that I couldn't have wrapped my
arms around if I'd tried. Hedges in front had been trimmed into
the shape of the letters ACCC, probably the country club's
initials, and manicured lawns stretched out behind it, the grass
perfectly even and lusciously green despite the heat.

Instead of pulling into the circle drive, I coasted past the
club and parked in the lot at the side. It wasn't so much that I
was embarrassed to park my twenty year old Suburban in front
of such a fancy establishment, more that there wasn't any space
left underneath the overhang. Three catering vans were parked

there, as well as a florist's van and a huge pickup truck with a trailer attached to it.

With the truck situated in the shade of a tall pine, Dawn, Tank, and I hopped out and headed up the walkway toward the club. Chefs in white smocks shuffled back and forth between their vans and the entrance unloading racks packed with trays. A valet stand stood unoccupied near the front double doors, but I didn't expect anyone to be working it yet. There were still a few hours until the event was scheduled to begin.

I let Dawn lead the way inside, though she didn't know where we were going any better than I did. A florist in stained overalls pushed past us as we stepped into the cool conditioned air, weaving to avoid bumping us with the fronds hanging from the edge of an oversized vase. The racks clanked and clattered as the chefs wheeled them in, and someone in a darker smock shouted at them from down the hallway to bring the meats in next.

I gathered alongside Dawn and Tank next to a round table at the center of the entryway. Although people were in no short supply, they all appeared to have their orders. "Who were we supposed to meet again, Dawn?"

"Her name is Olivia Something-or-other. Last name started with an h, I think. Hey. You." Dawn pointed at the nearest chef, a short Hispanic man with a thin mustache. "Do you know who's in charge here?"

I think the guy understood English, though how much was in question. He gestured toward the banquet hall and nodded, muttering something incomprehensible.

Dawn headed further in, and I followed. The banquet hall was less hectic than the entryway, with barely a soul waltzing among the linen clad tables and padded chairs. There was one guy there, a young man who was probably my junior, dressed in a crisp white shirt, dark grey pants, and a matching suit jacket. The getup made me conscious of my shorts, halter top, and flip-flops. Country clubs had dress codes, didn't they? At least Dawn and Tank weren't any more dressed up than I was.

"Excuse me," said Dawn. "We're looking for Olivia?"

The kid smiled and nodded, as polite as could be. "Last time I saw her she was in the ballroom. Down the hall to your right." He pointed.

We followed his instruction. Sure enough, where the banquet hall funneled us into a hall, a door branched out into another large room with cocktail tables in the corners. Half of them had already been adorned with flowers, and the florist we'd previously brushed past was placing his load on one of them. A woman in a tight beige skirt and an airy white blouse stood beside him, giving instructions. "Yes, in the back. We might need to find some wider tables. Those centerpieces are larger than I expected."

"Excuse me," said Dawn. "Are you Olivia...?"

"Hargreaves, yes." She waved the florist toward the back. "Put it over there for now. Can I help you?"

"I'm Dawn Blayde. This is Lexie Rodriguez and Tank John-son. We're with the Nyte Patrol."

"Ah." A relieved smiled crossed the woman's face as she came to greet us. "It's so good of you to make it. I apologize for calling on such short notice. I'm aware of the strain that puts on you from an organizational standpoint. Anytime a wrench is thrown into my plans, I feel like I'm going to have a heart attack until I get everything ironed out."

I don't think she was lying. Despite the tight bun that held her hair and her general look of togetherness, there was obvious tension in Olivia's face, and the creases in her brow hadn't smoothed upon meeting us.

"Do you mind getting us up to speed?" asked Dawn. "We need to know exactly what sort of service you're hoping for us to provide."

Olivia flicked a hand at the florist as he stepped past us into the hall. "The yellow one next, please. Thank you. Sorry. What we're hosting tonight is a fundraiser for the museum. It's not precisely an annual event. It's dependent upon the exhibits that come in on loan, but the organizers try to have at least one every year. If you don't woo the donors with some level of frequency, they tend to find other causes to devote their money to. We've had the gala at the museum in the past, but this year the organizers wanted to do something a little different, which is of course making my life more difficult." Olivia shrugged. "What can you do? Part of my job is to roll with the punches."

"And this is for the natural history museum downtown, right?" I said.

"That's correct."

I glanced at Dawn, my brow furrowed. "Ms. Hargreaves, I don't mean to be rude, but do you know what we specialize in? We're not a security company, per se. We're more of a consulting and detective firm—a *supernatural* one."

Olivia nodded primly, seemingly unoffended. "Oh, I'm very aware. That's precisely why I called."

Dawn looked as confused as I did. "It is?"

"Of course. History is the study of the past. It's a search for truth, and the true nature of natural history is fundamentally paranormal. It's the history of witches and wizards, of vampires and werefolk and the fae as much as it is one of dinosaurs and plate tectonics."

Olivia caught me off guard with the information. Dawn recovered more quickly than I did. "But none of that stuff is showcased in the museum."

"Not in the portions accessible to the public," said Olivia. "You have to know who to talk to to see the full exhibits. Speaking of which, if you could move please."

The woman ushered us to the side of the ballroom. I'd anticipated the florist returning with another overflowing vase, but it was a pair of movers pushing an enormous crate on a dolly.

Olivia waved at the box. "That's the newest item on loan from the natural history museum in Ottawa. A Sasquatch skeleton, found preserved in the Canadian tundra roughly twenty years ago. The paleontologists who put it together suspect it's at least twenty thousand years old. Let's set it up in the middle of the room, gentlemen! Thank you!"

I blinked, still processing the fact that there was another museum underneath the regular museum with a bunch of magical artifacts squirreled away in it. I guess it shouldn't have surprised me. There was a secret lava cavern underneath the Harry Ransom Center, after all.

"So this is a supernatural gala, then?" I asked.

Olivia nodded. "We'll have all manner of guests here. Magic users. Different races. People with different... *specialties,* shall we say. One of our most generous donors is Baron Kornhäusel. He helped establish several of the major museums in Nuremberg before moving here at the start of World War I."

I assumed Baron Kornhäusel wasn't human as opposed to being unbelievably ancient. Hopefully he hadn't been friends with Ivan Romanov before we killed him. "Well, that makes more sense. But we should be honest with you, Ms. Hargreaves —we're not specifically a security firm. We've worked small jobs, but never anything of this magnitude." *And never without Larry at our side,* I left unsaid.

Olivia blushed. "I'm so sorry. I thought I'd made that clear. We only need you to provide *supernatural* security for the event. We contracted another company to provide the regular security weeks ago, but the organizers called me early this morning insisting we needed something more comprehensive. They suggested you, hence the short notice. Once again, I'm so glad you could make it."

"Another comp—" I didn't even finish the word before I spotted a familiar gigantic oaf clad in black tromp around the edge of the doorway.

Otis pulled his aviator sunglasses off and smiled at us. "Well. Fancy seeing you guys again."

20

DAWN AND I STARED AT OTIS. I TRIED TO KEEP THE annoyance off my face, but Dawn didn't manage to keep her blatant disgust hidden at all. "Let me guess. You contracted with BSI for tonight's gala."

"In the flesh." Otis spread his arms wide as he approached, the mirrored sunglasses dangling from the fingers of his right hand. "Olivia, you didn't tell me you'd invited the Nyte Patrol to tag along."

"Hello, Otis." The woman nodded cordially. "Good to see you. And yes, Ms. Blayde. BSI has managed security for our galas for years. We wouldn't think to hire anyone else, not with the fine job they've done for us in the past. It's my fault for not contacting you, Otis. I received instructions to hire the Nyte Patrol this morning, and you know how busy things get the day of. My apologies. I hope your working together won't be a problem."

"Not on our end," said Otis. "We're always willing to mentor others, no matter how small or inexperienced their organization might be."

Tank hadn't said much, or really anything since arriving at the country club, but he crossed his arms and growled. Olivia picked up on it, because she laughed nervously as she smiled.

"Excellent. Well... Otis, perhaps you can familiarize them with some of your operations. In the meantime I should, ah..." She looked around, eyes falling on the workers opening the crate with the Sasquatch remains inside. "You two. I thought I told you I wanted the skeleton at the end of the ballroom. We need to let as many people see it as possible. Not many will want to gaze at its back." She shot us the same forced smile. "I'm sorry. I need to see to this. If you have any questions, don't hesitate to ask. In the meanwhile, if you'll excuse me..."

Olivia scuttled away, leaving the three of us squaring off against Otis. To his credit, the big gump didn't back down. He stood there, his smile never wavering.

Dawn waited until Olivia was mostly out of range before opening up her ice valve. "What do you want, Otis? Is stealing one of our jobs not enough for you? Gotta take 'em all?"

"*Steal?*" Otis tried to look shocked as he tucked his glasses on the collar of his shirt. "In case you weren't listening, we were hired to provide security weeks ago. You got called this morning, it sounds like. Who's stealing whose job, again?"

I didn't feel the same ire toward Otis that Dawn did, but I didn't like his smug arrogance, or the fact that he clearly thought we were beneath him. "You could've called to let us know you caught the thing that broke into Nine Moons. Ever heard of professional courtesy?"

Otis cocked his head at me, still smiling. "I don't see how that's my responsibility. Seems like maybe the owner should've done that. And instead of complaining, perhaps you should've put more of your efforts toward solving the case... unless that wasn't possible for you guys. Speaking of which, how are things? You keeping up on calls?"

"Go screw yourself, Otis." Dawn took me by the arm. "Let's get out of here. We don't need this asshole's help to prepare for tonight."

Otis chuckled as we headed toward the door, but he called out before we made it to the hall. "Hey, how's Larry? Getting any better?"

I turned, my annoyance finally shifting towards anger. "That's none of your business."

Otis shrugged, his fat jiggling. "Maybe not, but seems to me the people hiring you—the ones who want you to provide supernatural protection for their guests tonight—might want an *actual wizard* on duty rather than a drunk man-bear, a failed fitness model, and a wannabe hedge witch."

My face flushed. I took a step forward, but something stopped me. It wasn't Dawn either. She'd let go, but Tank had grabbed ahold.

His face was blank as slate, but there was a current of malice below the surface. "Let it go," he said softly. "He's not worth it."

He was right, even if I didn't want to admit it. Before I let the situation get out of hand, I turned and stormed toward the front of the club, Dawn and Tank hot on my heels.

I didn't keep my anger bottled in long. Barely had I made it out the front doors before I growled, my fists clenched into tight balls. "GOD that guy is an ass."

"Didn't realize it until now?" asked Dawn.

I shook my head angrily. "I thought he was just a jerk. Big difference."

The afternoon sun beat on my neck as we walked back to the car. Tank clapped me on the back. "You can't let dudes like that get to you. Bullies get pleasure out of negative reactions. If they see you get blue in the face, they're more likely to do it again."

"Why do you think I walked away when I did?"

Tank smirked. "You're really going to take all the credit, are you?"

I snorted. "Fair enough. Thanks. It's good to have you back by the way. You're already making a difference."

Tank nodded as we reached the truck. "Lets get back to the house. We need to get ready if we're going to do this job justice. That and I desperately need a nap."

We all hopped in. The Suburban roared and lurched as I pulled it into the street. Tank didn't make it more than two miles before I heard his soft snoring coming from the back.

I glanced at him in the rearview. Dawn noticed. "It's fine. Let him sleep."

"I was going to. I think he finally got it through his thick skull that we need him as much as he needs us. He's been pushing himself to the brink today to show he cares."

We drove in silence for a minute or two, the radio blaring softly in the background.

"Are you okay, Lexie?"

I cast her a quick glance as I pulled onto the highway. "Yeah. Sure."

I don't think reading minds was one of Dawn's super abilities, but she made a run at it anyway. "Tank's right you know. Otis is a dick. Ignore him."

I sighed. "But what if he's right?"

"About what? He was bullshitting us."

"About us being in over our heads. About them being able to

muscle us out. All the crap he was insinuating if not necessarily saying out loud."

"Relax, Lexie," said Dawn. "It'll be easier now that Tank's back in the fold. We'll get through to Larry soon enough. With everyone back together, we'll make it work. The money will flow, we'll pay off our debts, and we'll build a following along the way just so we can cram Otis's foot into his mouth."

"But what about tonight? We've never provided security for anything."

"It's a gala for a museum. We'll patrol the area and watch for party crashers. It's in our name, for Christ's sake. The Nyte *Patrol*. Don't worry. Nothing's going to go wrong."

21

I STOOD BESIDE THE COUNTRY CLUB'S FRONT DOORS, ON THE opposite side from the valet station and as out of the way as I could manage. Stars twinkled in the night sky above, but heat lingered in the air, slicking my skin with sweat and making my shirt stick to my chest. I'd had to change out of my shorts and flip-flops for more professional attire, which in this case meant a plain black shirt and matching pants. I wish we'd gone for something more unique, because the attire made us look exactly like the folks from BSI, minus the black combat boots, bulletproof vests, and utility belts, of course. I think they wore them to try and look badass, because I wasn't sure armor designed to deflect bullets would do a lot of good against the things they'd find themselves up against if everyone at the party suddenly decided to abandon the rule of law.

I'd stood near the front doors more or less since sundown, and the sheer variety of beings who'd pulled up and unfolded out of their rides hadn't stopped surprising me. There were the folks who were plainly not human: the flock of pint-sized pixies who'd swarmed out of the gull-wing doors of a Tesla Model X, the three foot tall gnome wearing a pointed red hat and with hairy feet bare, and a humanoid creature with a dog's head and hands that were two sizes too big. Then there were the folks who were *mostly* human, the pale-skinned vampire who poured out of a black stretch limo surrounded by a gaggle of attractive, vacuous young women in too-short dresses, the gray-haired woman who walked with a feline grace and obvious lightness of foot, and the robe-clad old codger whose white beard trailed the floor. But the ones who put me the most on edge were the ones I couldn't peg. One young man who drove up in a red Ferrari wearing a black tuxedo had eyes that were completely white, the iris, the pupil, everything, and another woman who chose to walk to the club rather than drive must've been seven and half-feet tall and weighed well over four hundred pounds. Even now, with sounds of revelry behind me, new party guests continued to arrive, and all of them, even the most normal-looking, carried about them magical auras. I don't think my senses had dulled since the morning, but it was hard to tell given the strengths of the Smells I detected. Honeysuckle, a simian body funk, wet paper, burnt rubber, Smell after Smell without any rhyme or reason to why they were attached to certain individuals. Maybe someday it would make sense to me.

"Excuse me? Miss?"

I turned to find the young man who'd earlier pointed us toward Olivia Hargreaves standing in the same suit as before, a tray of *hors d'oeuvres* that had mostly been picked clean in hand.

"Hi," I said.

He smiled sheepishly and lifted his tray. "Thought I might see if you were hungry. Working these events can be rough. Luckily, nobody in the kitchen minds if you snag a few morsels to keep your energy up. They're in the same boat, after all."

I smiled. I knew what the young man was up to, but I was surprised he had the courage to make a move. I was pretty sure he was still in high school. "You host a lot of events like these at the country club?"

"Oh, I don't work for the club," he said. "I work for the catering company. Out of This World Eats. We do a lot of events for supernatural folk."

"So that's why you haven't had a heart attack and died, yet."

He shrugged. "My dad's a warlock, so I got exposed to this stuff at a young age. It's all old hat by now, though there's always somebody who shows up who throws me for a loop."

I thought about the guy with the dog head and the huge hands. "You can say that again." I grabbed one of the remaining mushroom tarts from the tray and popped it in my mouth. "Thanks."

The young man smiled again, his wavy hair hanging haphazardly across his brow. "No problem. I could snag you a drink, too, if you want one."

I swallowed. "I shouldn't. Have to stay alert."

He nodded. "No problem. I'll, ah... see you around."

He retreated toward the club, glancing over his shoulder before reluctantly disappearing inside. What could I say? He wasn't my type, but I gave him credit for trying.

As I turned my attention back to the circle drive, my phone rang. I pulled it from my pocket and pulled it to my ear. "Hey."

"Hey," said Dawn. "Everything good?"

"Nothing of note to report," I said, "though I've enjoyed my fair share of people watching. You want to trade spots?"

"I get to enjoy the same view from where I am, don't you worry. Any chance you've seen Tank recently?"

I felt silly talking on my phone. The BSI folks all had

earpieces. "Not since we split up after our briefing. How come?"

"He's supposed to be making his rounds, same as me. I haven't seen him in at least twenty minutes."

"Maybe he's taking a nap."

"Another one?"

"Well, I don't know," I said. "I told you we should've gotten walkie-talkies. Would've made this a lot easier." For reasons that had to do with his arkoúdathropy, Tank didn't carry a cell phone. He'd spend too much replacing it each time he turned and lost it.

"Yeah, well, hindsight is twenty-twenty. Do you think you could abandon the front for a few minutes? I'd like to make sure he didn't wander off."

"You think he'd do that?"

"He was drunk and in jail earlier this morning," said Dawn. "I'd like to believe he's turned a corner, but you leave him alone, in the dark. Maybe he swipes a few cocktails off a tray..."

"Got it," I said. "I'll take a look. What side of the club are you on?"

"The west."

"Alright. I'll loop around the east."

I stuffed the phone into my pocket and headed off along the sidewalk. Instead of taking it toward the parking lot, I stepped onto the path that curved along the side of the golf club. Floodlights at the corners of the building cast yellow cones of light between the trees onto the neatly trimmed bushes and the crunching gravel underfoot. A steady hum of music and conversation drifted through the air, muted into a constant background by the club's walls. Somewhere in the grass, crickets chirped and birds trilled.

I turned a corner toward the back patio and nearly slammed face first into a party guest. I recoiled. "Oh my gosh. I'm so sorry. I..."

It took me that long to realize the person I'd nearly bowled over wasn't a guest. It was one of BSI's employees, decked out in full riot gear, minus the helmet.

He gave me a brusque nod. "Watch where you're going."

The guy couldn't have been more than a few years older than me. He had a fresh face, feathery chestnut locks, high cheekbones, a strong jaw. Amazing how a simple gruff interjection and the emblem on his chest could completely kill any feelings of attraction I might've had under other circumstances. Suddenly, the kid with the *hors d'oeuvres* didn't seem half bad.

"Sorry," I said again. "I didn't see you. Comes with wearing all black, I guess."

He snorted and planted his hands on his hips, one of them unnervingly close to the pistol that hung here. "You're blocking my patrol route."

I'd already said sorry twice. I wasn't about to offer a third apology. I also didn't move out of the way. "Have you seen a big black guy wandering around back here? About six foot six, not quite three bills."

The young man frowned. "What?"

"He works with us," I said.

"*Us?*" The guy gave me a blank look.

"The Nyte Patrol?" I said. "You know we're working this job, too, right? My partner said she hasn't seen—"

The floodlights cut out, plunging us into darkness. I looked up toward the windows on the floor above us, but those too had gone dark. Similarly, the music playing inside had also stopped, which in turn helped me better hear a slew of gasps and murmurs of discontent from the partiers.

"What the..." The BSI guard's hand flew to his comm unit, activating the device plugged in his ear. "This is Weeks. Everything okay in there?"

I heard a faint crackle from the earpiece, but I couldn't make anything specific out. "What's going on?"

The guy waved at me to hush. "Probably a fuse. Someone's going to check the circuit breaker. Seriously, don't you have anything better to do than bother me?"

A bloodcurdling scream cut through the air, causing me to take a step back from the building. A resounding crash quickly followed, followed by another—the sound of heavy timbers cracking and snapping.

"Jesus Christ! A fuse, was it?"

Another scream sounded, followed by a series of panicked cries. Then the unmistakable crack of a gunshot smashed my eardrums. It came from inside.

The BSI guard whirled toward the stairs. "Shit!"

A patio door slammed open, and someone else in a bullet-proof vest and with a pistol in hand leaned over the railing. "Weeks! Get the hell in here, *now!"*

22

Despite his fancy tactical gear, I had the better reflexes. I pushed past Weeks and darted toward the stairs, taking them two at a time up to the patio. The guy who'd yelled at my new BSI acquaintance flicked on his flashlight, sending a beam of light cutting through the darkness. Another one flicked on behind me, and once I reached the windows, I could see a few more arcing across the ceiling inside the club. People continued to scream. A few folks in gowns and suits burst out the patio door, their faces drawn and eyes wide. Something whisked by me through the air as I tried to push past them in the opposite direction, whether sprite or bat or oversized dragonfly I couldn't tell.

Another crash sounded as I surged inside, the club shaking under my feet from the force of the blow. Something roared, a guttural, animalistic sort of noise, but I couldn't tell where it had come from. I'd toured the club before the party started to familiarize myself with the layout, but in the darkness, with the roars and screams reverberating off the walls, I couldn't remember where I was much less tell where the sounds were coming from.

Weeks and his BSI partner flew in behind me, flashlights and pistols in hand. They screamed at each other over the commotion.

"What the hell is going on?" asked Weeks.

"Beats the hell out of me," said the other. "The lights went out and the next thing I know people started screaming."

"Where?" I asked.

They both looked at me as if wondering why I'd bothered asking them. As I waited on a response, I felt a rush of air and caught a blur of motion out of the corner of my eye. I turned, another flashlight's bright white cone sweeping across a portion of the room at the end of the hall. A glimpse of a familiar yellow floral arrangement caught my eye, followed immediately by a crystalline clatter, dozens if not hundreds of brittle snaps and cracks.

I immediately knew where I was. "The ballroom."

I rushed forward, bursting through the doors as another couple guests ran past me in the opposite direction. Even in the darkness, it looked as if a whirlwind had passed through. A single cocktail table stood upright. The others had all been knocked to the floor, the vases and flowers they'd held shattered and scattered across the hardwood, and the prized Sasquatch skeleton, which I'd only seen in passing during my tour, lay smashed to pieces alongside them.

My phone buzzed angrily in my pocket, but I ignored it. Cones of light streamed like spotlights across the adjoining hall. I heard a wet thump and a cry. Someone in BSI gear flew through the hallway, landing on their back with a sickening crunch.

It wasn't until then that I acknowledged the fear coursing

through me, but rather than run, rather than freeze in place, I paused, focused, and opened myself to magic.

I'd practiced it hundreds of times now, some with Larry before he stopped talking to me but mostly on my own. Practicing with potions, wards, enchantments, and summoning circles. I hadn't practiced opening myself to the flow of magic with my life on the line, but the energies nonetheless surged into me. I felt an energy in the air that I could tap into to summon fire or lightning. Colors seemed richer, darks darker, the spaces illuminated by the roaming flashlights brighter. Auras popped into existence around me, as did Smells, including that of... *licorice.*

It was unmistakable. Like the one I'd smelled at Nine Moons but fresher. Had BSI brought the duende here? If so, why?

I didn't have time to think about it, as another BSI guard slid across the hallway in front of me, groaning as he did so. The screams from further in the building had been replaced by shouts of rage, but the action sounded close. With a firm grip on the magical energies around me, I burst out of the ballroom, around the corner, and into the reception hall.

I skidded to a halt and froze at the scene in front of me.

It was Tank. *In bear form.*

A half dozen BSI goons surrounded him, some with flashlights, others holding guns. A pair of electrical leads trailed his furry hide to a discarded taser. Tank reared and roared, massive paws held high. The goons shouted at him, waving their guns and shining their flashlights. One of them lifted a can of mace and unleashed a torrent of pepper spray into his face. Tank's roar turned from one of rage to pain. His paws slammed the floor. He pushed off with his powerful back legs and dove through the two nearest flunkies, sending them flying into nearby tables.

I finally managed to get a grip on myself. I darted forward, hands held out. "Tank! *Stop it! Calm down!*"

At this point, I was in the dark both physically and figuratively. I didn't know what was going on. I didn't know what had triggered Tank to turn, what had started the fight between him and BSI, or who had thrown the first punch. I didn't know why the lights had cut out, if it was Tank who had trashed the ballroom, if there were any party guests left in harm's way, or if there was more fighting between BSI and Dawn and parties unknown outside. All I knew was that Tank was in danger and he was being assaulted.

Which is why it was so surprising when Tank's eyes landed on me without an ounce of care, compassion, or recognition in them.

I blinked, feeling as if I'd been slapped. When Tank turned into a Kodiak, he lost some of his ability for rational thought. He lost his ability for speech, and the bear instincts inside him threatened to take over. But he didn't lose *everything*. At least, he'd never lost it before.

I took a step forward. "Tank? Are you...?"

Tank growled and rushed me with unbelievable speed. If I'd let go of my magic, I would've been defenseless. As it was, I managed to get my hands up in time to unleash the first thing that came to mind. The easiest and one of the first spells I'd learned to cast. A fireball.

It wasn't the right choice. The fire erupted from my palms, screaming toward Tank, but it didn't force him to stop or turn or even lift a giant arm to protect his face. He was too close and moving too fast already.

The gout of fire crashed off his face and chest, half of it bouncing onto the ceiling and the other half flying back toward me. I twisted just in time as the flames reversed course, but it was the bear missile that smashed into me that got me out of their clutches faster.

I grunted as I took the full weight of Tank's blast in the side. I felt my feet leave the ground, felt myself fly through the air, wind whistling past my ears. I tried to think, tried to keep hold of the magic in my grip, but the pain blossoming through me made it hard to focus on anything else. I felt like I'd been pegged with a fastball.

A new wave of pain arced through my body as I smashed into a wall, and I crumpled to the floor. The magic fled my grasp, as did my ability to think, see, or even stay conscious. Darkness and flashing lights swam in my vision. I blinked, or at least I think I did, but in the span of that fraction of a second, the environment changed around me. The room was lighter, brighter, warmer. The lights above me hadn't come back on, and yet something had changed.

I groaned as I rolled onto my back. Above me, flames danced along the walls, rippling along drapes until they found the ceiling. The flames shimmered and shook, a sea of orange and yellow revelers waving in chaotic unison.

A new roar filled my ears, but it wasn't that of a bear, nor was it the roar of angry shouts. More of a pervasive background. The roar of an ocean. The roar of high winds. The fire, perhaps? It was soothing in a way. Ocean sounds always were, otherwise they wouldn't be sold on CDs to old people who had trouble sleeping. Come to think of it, sleep sounded pretty good about now.

My eyelids crept downward, feeling heavy. Maybe a nap would do me well. It was so warm, so comfortable, the pain that I'd felt a moment ago dulled to a smooth background.

"Lexie? Lexie!"

I groaned as I heard the call. I reached for my phone, trying to pluck it from my pocket. "Give me a sec... I'm coming." The words sounded more jumbled in my ears than I'd intended.

As I fumbled at my pocket, a face appeared in my vision. A dream of exotic beauty, except this one was real. *"Dawn?"*

"Lexie! Thank God. We've got to go. Now!"

I groaned. "Later. I'm tired. Give me a minute."

"What?" Dawn looked as if she hadn't understood. "Lexie, this place is coming down! The fire—"

Something creaked and crashed. Dawn ducked and bobbed to the side. I felt the rumble of vibration through my back, and something tickled my throat. Dust? Smoke?

Dawn shook me by the shoulders. "Lexie, we don't have time for this. Can you move?"

"I... Ah..." I wiggled my fingers and toes, but my arm seemed to have gone numb, not to mention I couldn't think straight.

"Damnit. Forget it!" Dawn leaned over. Her arms dug underneath me. I felt her lean, corded muscle wrap around me, felt the pinch of her fingers as they grasped my thigh and shoulder—ah, there was the arm. It wasn't totally numb then.

Dawn grunted with the effort, but she turned and stumbled out of the room. As she did so, the world turned around me, and I got a glimpse at the lounge. Fire licked three of the four walls, having also spread to the tables and chairs nearest them. One of the BSI folks lay cradling his arm while a pair of his buddies forced him to his feet. Past them a hole the size of a pickup truck had punched through the wall to the darkness outside. Smoke boiled through it, wafting up to the twinkling stars beyond. Of Tank, there was no sign.

I still didn't have my wits about me, but it was about then that I realized things had maybe taken a turn for the worse.

23

Dawn drove the Suburban while I rested as best as I could in the passenger seat. The simple fact that she was willing to get behind the wheel said everything about my current condition. It wasn't that I couldn't move. Although I'd initially thought my arm might've been broken, the feeling slowly crept back into it, along with a dull pain that made me suspect my entire body would be a bruise come two days from now. Rather it was the fact that I still couldn't totally think straight. Paramedics had rolled up to the parking lot of the club as we tore out, the flaming husk of the country club burning merrily in the rear-view mirror. We could've stayed and spoken with them. Medically-speaking, that would've been the smart choice, even if I didn't think I had a concussion. Then again, getting the hell out of dodge before anyone starting asking too many questions was probably smarter, especially given the last conversation we'd had with Frank Connors.

Dawn hunched over the wheel, looking like she'd slammed half a dozen shots of espresso. It might've been the adrenaline, but I think the nerves at having to drive for the first time in a decade had something to do with it, too. "Shit shit *shit.*"

"Yeah, this is decidedly not good." I could still see the glow of the fire brightening the night sky behind us. "We have a liability insurance policy, don't we?"

"An insurance policy?" Dawn glared at me. "Jesus, are you worried about the *fire?*"

"Aren't you? I'm the one who cast the fireball that set the place ablaze. The building is probably worth ten million. We can't cover that. We can't even keep up on our mortgage."

"First of all, do not tell *anyone* you're the one who cast that spell," said Dawn. "That place was a fucking madhouse. No one knows what the hell happened. Everyone's going to have a different story. Second of all, the fire is the least of our worries. Lexie, that was *Tank* in there."

"Hello? I know. I'm the one he body slammed into the wall. What the hell happened, Dawn? Who threw the first punch? Why did Tank turn? Who smashed up the ballroom?"

Dawn's eyes were wide. Strained. "You mean you didn't see it either?"

My head hurt. Thinking was hard. "What do you mean, *either?*"

Dawn swore. "I don't know. I was outside when the lights went out. I hadn't seen Tank since before I called you. As soon as the lights died, I heard a scream and a crash and I rushed inside to find a bunch of those BSI nut jobs with their guns drawn. They were yelling at me to get back, and I was yelling back at them. Long story short one of them put his hands on me and had a bad day. By the time I got myself free, all hell had broken loose. People were getting out of the club as fast as they could. None of them would tell me what was going on.

Guess they didn't know. It was dark as hell in there. By the time I worked my way to the reception area, Tank was being mauled by BSI agents and you were on the ground, seeing stars."

"So you missed the fireball, too?"

"I told you, shut up about the fireball. You didn't cast any magic, got it? What did you see?"

I shrugged and instantly regretted it. My neck was not happy. "I was in the same boat as you. I missed what started it. I came into the brawl maybe a minute before you did. Tank couldn't have instigated it, right? It had to be those BSI jerks who attacked first."

"I have no idea," said Dawn, "but regardless of whether or not anyone noticed your fire magic, there's bound to be dozens of witnesses who saw the giant Kodiak bear smashing things and attacking people before busting an enormous hole in the wall and running off. Now we don't even know where he is. *Fuck!*"

I took a deep breath. I was feeling the faintest bit nauseous, but I could overcome it. "Dawn... He looked at me. Right before he attacked. I know he's not all there when he's in bear form, but it seemed like *none* of him was there. I'd never seen him like that before."

Dawn didn't seem to hear me. "We need to get in front of this. We need to find him and figure out what the hell happened before BSI and the cops descend on us."

She reached out and fumbled with the radio as she took a ramp onto the expressway about ten miles too fast. The Suburban shuddered and leaned dangerously to the right, the wheels squealing. I think the left side lifted off the ground for a fraction of a second.

"Christ! You sure you don't want me to drive?"

Dawn waved at the radio. "I'll be fine. How the hell do you tune this thing?"

"What station do you want?"

"Mystic Radio."

The AM and FM channels were easy enough to get, but as a station that focused on supernatural news and entertainment, Mystic Radio ran along a different wavelength, one transmitted on waves outside the regular electromagnetic spectrum. Larry had fiddled with my car radio months ago and done something to allow it to pick up the station. I hadn't really known what until I'd learned some magic myself.

I latched hold of the magical energies around me as I took hold of the radio dial. After a few seconds of fiddling, the thing crackled and a full-bodied radio voice cut in. "—and the fire, as far as we know, is still raging. Are firefighters on the scene? My producer Mick is shaking his head no. I don't know if that means they're not there, or we don't know. No word? He's saying we don't have word, folks."

Silence filled the air for a moment before another voice, somewhat higher pitched but with that wacky tenor that worked for morning shows, responded. "Ok, folks, we're tracking this story as best we can for you. Obviously, it's unfolding as we speak. For those of you just tuning in, we've got breaking news. Something attacked tonight's gala at the Arbor Crest Country Club. We don't know what happened, exactly, but the attendees were forced to flee for their lives. Gunshots were fired and magic spells cast. The golf club is currently going up in flames, but we don't know how many supers or mundies were hurt or killed, if any. Do we, Mick?"

A third voice came onto the mike amid a shuffling of papers.

This one decidedly did not have a voice for radio. "We don't know, Marty."

"Okay. Well, this is some crazy stuff folks. I know you're used to us delivering the news as raw and unfiltered as we can, so that's what we're going to do, but we're also not used to events of this magnitude unfolding. The good news is that, as far as we know, nobody has been seriously injured. *As far as we've heard.* Just want to reiterate that. Okay, Turk's waving at me. What have you got, buddy?"

The first full-bodied voice spoke. "Apparently, we've got a caller on the phone, Marty. Someone who says they were at the party. Line one, you're on the air."

A new voice sprouted from the speaker, one muffled and crackly from the phone reception. The person spoke with a heavy German accent. *"Ya? Hallo?* Is zis Marty and Turk with ze Truth Squad?"

"In the flesh," said Marty. "What can you tell us, pal? Were you at the gala?"

"Ya, I vas. It vas terrible, let me tell you. So much chaos. None of us knew vat vas going on, ya? It was quite ze debacle."

I wondered if it was Baron Whatshisface, the guy Olivia had mentioned. Marty continued. "So you were there when it started?"

"Ya. I vas inside, speaking to my good friend Elliot Spiegel. Ve had just finished our second glass of *wein* when ze lights cut out. Zat's when—"

"Sorry, pal," said Turk. "I hate to cut you off. Please stay on the line if you can, we'd love to hear more from you in a second, but our producer just told me we've got another caller that we *have* to take. Caller two, Jane, are you there?"

I sucked in air as her voice floated through the airways, cool and haughty as always. "Hello Turk. Marty. Yes, I'm here. Jane Fettercross. Co-founder of Brute Squad Incorporated."

"Thank you for calling, Jane," said Marty. "As you know, we've been flooded with information tonight. Your firm, BSI, was providing security to the gala, isn't that right?"

"That's correct, Marty," said Jane. "We'd been co-contracted with another firm, one by the name of the Nyte Patrol. I believe you might've heard of them?"

"Oh, we've heard of them," said Marty. "We covered that business with the ghosts and the O'Neills extensively on our show a few weeks ago."

Jane's voice turned frostier, if possible. "Yes. It wasn't our choice, but we've always been happy to work with other contractors at the request of our clients. The reason I'm calling, however, is because even though I wasn't at tonight's gala, I've spoken to several of my operatives who were there, including my husband and co-owner Otis, and I think I can shed light on what happened."

"By all means," said Turk. "We've been stubbing our toes in the dark here, sifting through conflicting eye witness accounts. In your official capacity as event security, *what actually happened?*"

"It doesn't give me any pleasure to say this, but my employees and numerous other party guests have confirmed it. The individual responsible for the attacks at Arbor Crest is none other than Nyte Patrol employee Tank Johnson."

Dawn growled. *"That bitch..."*

"My men and women spotted him sneaking drinks meant for guests and starting to stumble. When they confronted him, he became agitated and belligerent. They told him to leave and get himself sober, but instead he attacked them. He turned, right then and there. He endangered the lives of hundreds during his wild attacks."

"So you're saying this Nyte Patrol member was *drunk on the job?*" said Marty.

"Yes. And it's worse, because my sources tell me he was released from jail this very morning for public intoxication and disorderly conduct."

My eyes shot open. "What the hell? How did she know that?"

"Someone like this, an addict, in that condition, should never have been allowed on the premises tonight," continued Jane. "He endangered not only himself but everyone in that building. He set the place afire, he attacked my employees, one of which is headed to the hospital, he caused millions of dollars in property damage, and now he's loose in west Austin in bear form. This man is a menace, but the supernatural community can rest easy, because I can guarantee the both of you, we're going to find him. We're going to track him down and bring him to justice. We take our employment and our business seriously, and we refuse to let some angry, drunk, reckless man-child—"

Dawn roared and slammed a hand against the radio, shutting if off. The car shuddered as Dawn braked suddenly, moving us onto an exit ramp. I gripped the armrest, feeling my adrenaline spike. "Dawn? You sure you don't want me to drive?"

The tires screeched as Dawn pulled off the highway onto FM 2222. "They're going to go after him, Lexie. That's what she's saying. He attacked their own and now they're going to take revenge. She's just laying down cover so when they kill him, they can claim it was in self-defense. Shit! This is even worse than I thought."

"Are you serious?" My mind raced. "Why would BSI go after Tank like that?"

"I don't know," said Dawn. "Probably because he attacked them, just like she said. They already didn't like us. Now this gives them an opportunity to crush us. Even if they don't find him and kill him, what's the alternative? That the cops find him and throw him in jail? You said Connors was at the end of his rope. This is it. One way or another, Tank is done for and so are we."

I took a deep breath as street signs flashed by. "Maybe not. Not if we find him first."

"And how the hell do you plan on doing that?"

I swallowed hard. "We'll need more help."

24

I KICKED OPEN THE BASEMENT DOOR AND STORMED DOWN the steps, Dawn hot on my heels. The space still glowed with the same orange glimmer I'd seen when I'd visited a few days ago. The light played off the exposed beams overhead, though the piles of ancient junk prevented me from seeing exactly where it was coming from.

"Larry!" I called. *"Larry!* Where are you?"

I heard a sigh deep within the cardboard box fort. "My answer hasn't changed, Lexie. Go away. I'm not interested."

"She's not the only one," called Dawn. "I'm here, too, and if you don't get your butt out here in the next ten seconds, I'm going to dive in, kick your ass, and pull you up the stairs, even if you're kicking and screaming all the way."

I heard a snort. "I figured both of you would be back sooner or later. Probably together. I get it. You're stubborn, but so am I. Just give up, already. Seriously. It's like eleven o'clock at night. I'm about ready to—"

I couldn't take it any longer. *"Tank is gone, Larry!"*

There was a shuffle, and Larry appeared through a gap in the boxes some twenty feet along the central aisle. "What do you mean he's gone?"

Heat radiated off Dawn. Her teeth squeaked as she unclenched them. "Unlike you, we've been working, Larry. We had a job tonight. A security detail. Tank went crazy. Got drunk and attacked some Brute Squad members. Apparently put one of them in the hospital. Then he ran off. Now BSI is after him, and the police will be too soon enough. Unless we get to him first."

Larry stepped forward, still wearing his leather duster. His skin was both paler and greener than it had been a few days ago, his beard longer and more matted. A putrid stench rolled off him, and I had to suppress a gag.

Larry's brow furrowed, the lines in his forehead floppier than they used to be. "So he just... ran off? Why didn't you stop him?"

"Why didn't we...!?!" Dawn practically fumed, her nostrils flaring. "Are you hearing yourself? Do you have *any idea* what's been going on above your head for the past week? Any idea the hours Lexie and I have put in? The state Tank's been in? The drinking? The drugs? Do you know how many calls we've gotten? Any idea how much we've got in the bank account? Do you? And you have the gall to ask why we didn't *do more,* while you've sat here hiding in the basement like a, like a..."

Dawn shook with anger. I reached out and grabbed her by the arm. "Dawn. Please. Let me."

She stood there, breathing heavily, staring daggers at Larry, but she gave me the slightest of nods.

I turned to face Larry, who already looked like he'd been slapped. "Larry. I'm sorry. I'm sorry for turning you into a zombie. It's my fault, and I take full responsibility for it. I know maybe that doesn't mean a whole lot, but I promise that if you let us in, I'll help you figure out a way to beat this disease. Dawn will help you. Bill will help, and Tank will, too, but first we have to find him. And that's the point. We need your help. Not just Tank. All of us. We can't do this—run the business, deal with the cops, fend off BSI—without your help. You've always been the glue keeping this group together, and I think if you look inside yourself, you'll see that you need our help, too. Just... give us a chance."

Larry stood there, listening intently the whole time. His eyebrows had drawn together, his dull eyes acquiring the faintest hint of a sparkle. As I finished my speech, he hung his head. When he spoke, it was in little more than a whisper. "I'm... sorry, too. I haven't been myself lately, quite literally, but that's not an excuse. Shutting you guys of all people out...? I guess I've been a pretty shitty business partner as well as friend."

Dawn was still breathing hard, but she was slowing down.

I didn't even have to swallow my revulsion as I reached out and touched his shoulder. "It's okay. We get it. Tank's been going through the same."

Larry nodded. "But fact of the matter is, I don't know how much I can help. I isolated myself down here in part to get away from you guys, but also to keep you from seeing what's happened to me. I've changed."

Dawn snorted, but it wasn't in derision. It was a familiar, friendly sort of snort. "We can tell. We have eyes. And noses."

"That's not what I mean," said Larry. "I mean, it is. Part of it anyway. But my magic isn't as strong as it used to be. This turning into a zombie business is messing with my ability to grab ahold of magical energies. I'll fight to the ends of the earth to protect any one of you, but if this business you're talking about with Tank puts us in a jam...?"

"Then leave the fighting to us," said Dawn. "We just need your help locating Tank. We've got to get to him before anyone else does."

I sighed. "We've gone over this a dozen times, Dawn. Larry can't track stuff via magic. Don't get me wrong, I think he could. When I made that magical Smell potion, I was able to track scents pretty well. With all the magical senses going, I bet he'd be able to track someone no problem, but that won't help us right now."

Larry lifted a gnarly brow. "You brewed a Smell potion? And you were able to use it to track scents?"

"Yeah. I know, right?"

A smile graced Larry's lips. "Nice." He shook his head. "But that's not important right now. Helping Tank is. Luckily, we may not need magic to find him. You said he went after the Brute Squad?"

"We're not sure if he started it, but yeah," said Dawn.

"Then at least that gives us somewhere to start. Might as well do it now. I've already swallowed my pride for the day."

"Pardon?" I said.

He nodded. "Come with me."

Larry pushed past us and headed up the stairs. Dawn and I followed him as he hooked a left at the top and walked into the living room. Bill was there, leaning against the side of his jar, looking at the TV. An attractive young woman with a KXAN microphone in hand stood in the country club's parking lot while the club blazed merrily behind her. The sound was off, but in between gaps in the closed captioning, I could read the ticker at the bottom of the screen. It said "Kitchen Fire Sparks Blaze at Local Golf Hotspot." Leave it to the media to find a plausible explanation for everything.

"Bill," said Larry. "I need your help."

Bill turned in his jar. "Larry! Holy crap, it's good to see you. You— Oh." Bill's eyes went wide.

"I know. I look like crap. Feel like crap, too. Comes with the territory, I guess."

Larry's face had started to sag, both physically and metaphorically. Bill smiled. "Hey, having a decaying body is better than having none at all. Take it from me. Besides, doesn't matter. I'm just glad you're out of the basement."

Larry cast me and Dawn an accepting glance. "Yeah. Me, too. Anyway, I need you to make a call. Put it through the speaker."

Bill's bluetooth headset lit up, despite the fact that he hadn't touched it or even banged it against the glass. I still wasn't sure how he did that. "You got it. Who do you want to call?"

"Otis Zachary Pacheco."

"Larry!" said Dawn. "You can't be serious?"

"Like I said, I'm swallowing my pride. Tank is worth it. All of you are." He gave Bill a nod.

Bill called out the number—I guess from memory—and the speakerphone system on Larry's giant desk rang.

Otis picked up on the third trill, his voice as oafish and deep as I remembered it. "Hello?"

"Otis. This is Larry Stuttgart."

"Larry. You've got a lot of nerve calling me given all that's happened tonight." Strangely enough, Otis didn't actually sound that cheesed. "Speaking of which, where were you at the gala? Still laid up with that thing that's been nagging you?"

"You know about what went down outside Lockhart?"

"I've heard rumors. And you seem to be conspicuously absent anytime I've run into your minions, which seems to be happening more often than I want it to."

"The feeling's mutual, Otis," said Dawn.

"Hey, the whole gang's there," said Otis. "Except for Tank, I have to assume. How's he doing? Has he turned back yet, or is he still out there murdering people and setting the city on fire?"

Larry stayed calm, despite the big guy's goads. "We're not looking to start a fight, Otis. In fact, I called to ask a favor."

"*A favor?* You do know what your boy Tank did at the club, don't you?"

"I do, but if what I've heard is accurate, you'd be smart to help us find him. I don't know what set him off, but when Tank gets enraged and turns, he can be extremely dangerous. You know that. Your guys went after him and didn't put a dent in him. Let us handle him. We can talk him down. Get him under control. No one else needs to get hurt, and the sooner we find him, the sooner we can make sure that's the case."

Otis laughed. He actually laughed, his powerful chuckle booming through the speaker.

Larry's voice cooled several degrees. "I'm not joking, Otis. I know you're looking for him. If you have a bead on him, tell us. It'll be best for everyone."

"You don't get it, do you?" said Otis.

"Let me take a guess," said Larry. "You want revenge? Tank put your employee in a hospital and now you want to see him pay?"

"*No,*" roared Otis. "My employees have health insurance. They know what they're getting into when they sign the contract. I don't give a rat's ass if one of them broke an arm or a collarbone. What I want is *you*."

"You mean Tank?" I said.

"All of you. Out of the picture. Austin's not big enough for the two of us, and *we* run the supernatural contracting racket around here. Your little stunt with the ghosts and the O'Neill's might've earned you a little notoriety, but I knew it wouldn't last. I knew it would backfire, and I've been foaming at the mouth waiting for it to do so. And now... BOOM. Your friend Tank goes and puts a couple hundred people in danger, burns down a golf club, and is on the run. You think I'm letting this go? I'm going to make sure *everyone* knows what happened. More than that, I hope he stays angry. I hope he stays dangerous, because I *like* dangerous. And I'm going to be the one to take him down, in full view of everyone. Say goodbye to those fat checks, because it's time for the Brute Squad to rise back on top. *For good."*

Larry sighed. "Otis..."

It was too late. The line clicked, and the dial tone sounded.

Dawn kicked the desk, sending it back a couple inches despite the weight. "God I hate that guy. I didn't even get a chance to tell him to fuck off before he hung up."

Larry reached out and tapped the end call button on the console. The fact that he was willing to touch the thing with his bare hand spoke to the degradation in his magical abilities. He used to be terrified of touching electronics for fear of making them explode. "Well, that could've gone better."

"No shit," said Dawn. "But we're better off not working with those assholes anyway. We'll find Tank on our own."

"Yeah?" said Larry. "How? In case you need a reminder,

we've been in this situation before. He's not easy to find. I mean, maybe if I can get the police to loan us a bloodhound again..."

"I think involving the police is a bad idea," I said. "We talked to Frank. Tank is on the thinnest of ice, and that was before tonight's events."

"Maybe we don't need a bloodhound," said Dawn. "Lexie, you said you were able to track scents from Nine Moons using that potion you crafted. You've smelled Tank, right? Magically speaking, of course. If you cook up another spell, you could track him."

I shrugged. "I mean, maybe. But that's going to take time, and there might be a simpler option. Larry, do you really think the Brute Squad has a clue where he might be?"

"You heard Otis," said Larry. "They think this is their chance to squash us. They've got way more technology and personnel on this than we do. I'd bet my life on it... or, you know what I mean."

"That's kind of what I thought, too," I said. "So all we need to do is tap into their communications."

Dawn blinked. "You know how to do that? Since when are you the techie in the group?"

"It shouldn't be that hard," I said. "Those ear pieces the BSI goons were wearing work off UHF bands, same as any other short range radio system. If we can get within range of them, all we should need is a walkie-talkie to listen in."

Larry nodded, his eyebrows drawing together. "You know what? That might work."

Bill hadn't said anything throughout the exchange, but his voice now warbled out of his jar. "Guys? We may not need the two-way radios at all."

"Why?" I asked.

He jutted his chin toward the TV, and we all turned and looked. The shot had switched from the young reporter in front of Arbor Crest County Club to a helicopter shot of a home. The ticker read "Bear Sighting at Police Commissioner's House."

My heart sank. "Oh, crap."

25

WE DIDN'T ACTUALLY KNOW WHERE THE POLICE commissioner lived, and the nighttime aerial shot shown on the news didn't help us narrow down the search. Luckily, we weren't totally inept either. Some googling and a quick call to one of Larry's private investigator friends later and we were on our way.

The Suburban shuddered as I pulled onto a residential street in Old West Austin, one lined by smallish homes from the fifties and sixties that had all probably been taken down to the studs and renovated before being flipped for well over a million dollars. The satellite image we'd pulled showed the commish's home was one of the larger ones, but we couldn't pull up in front of it. A police barricade had been set up about two and half houses down, yellow wooden barriers illuminated by a sea of portable lights, all of them connected to a generator on wheels that spewed electrical cords like squid tentacles.

I parked about ten feet from the edge of the barricade and put the car in park. There was only a single news truck on the scene, but it was parked across the barricade on the opposite side of the commissioner's house. That didn't mean all the attention was on the far side though. A flurry of uniformed officers huddled about the front of the commissioner's home, others swarmed their cars, the lights on top flashing red and blue, and a couple were waiting at the edge of the nearest barricade. Based on their stares, they clearly noticed us.

The engine sputtered as I pulled the keys from the ignition. "You sure about this, Larry? Frank made things pretty damn clear when we spoke this morning."

"We didn't want to involve the police, I grant you that," said Larry. "But Tank didn't give us much of a choice. We need to figure out where he is and make amends before this gets out of hand."

"I think it might already be there," mumbled Dawn as she popped her door.

We climbed out and approached the yellow sawhorses. The nearest officer held out a hand, his tone gruff. "Whoever you are, turn it around. Residents only, no exceptions."

"We need to talk to Frank Connors," said Larry. "Go find him. Tell him it's Larry Stuttgart. He'll come out."

The officer straightened his back and puffed his chest, taking a step toward the barricade. His gut bumped into it, threatening to knock it over. "I told you to turn it around, pal. Take another step toward me and I'll book you so damn fast you'll be seeing stars 'till next Tuesday."

Larry didn't take another step, but he didn't back up either. "Detective Frank Connors, head of the Special Investigations unit. You want to know why a bear rampaged through this neck of the woods? Better believe your commissioner wants to know, and so does Frank. If either of them hears you refused to tell them I arrived on the scene with information pertinent to the case, I'm not going to be the one whose ass is in a sling, I guarantee you."

The officer's nostrils flared. His cheeks puffed, but apparently Larry invoked the right names and used the right tone. The officer flicked an angry hand at the serviceman next to him. "Haynes. Keep an eye on these jokers. If they so much as sniff this barrier, you taze 'em, hear?"

The second officer nodded, his hand slipping to the tazer gun at his belt. He stared daggers at us as the overweight guy ambled off.

I tugged on Larry's sleeve, pulling him back from the edge of the barricade. I lowered my voice. "I'm telling you Larry, this is a bad idea. Frank made things crystal clear."

"He'll listen to me," said Larry. "He knows me. He might act tough, but underneath it all we're friends. And I'm the best source he's got. He wouldn't cut me off like that."

"He would if it's his job on the line," hissed Dawn. "You think he's going to put his neck on the chopping block for you when Tank just went after his boss?"

"Tank didn't do that," said Larry. "You're making things up. Why in the world would he attack the commissioner?"

"Beats the hell out of me," said Dawn. "But there's no reason he would've gone nuts and attacked the Brute Squad flunkies at the country club either. And if you think thirty cops have gathered here because the police commissioner simply *caught sight of* a bear, you've lost more than your magic while in the basement for the last two weeks."

"I'm telling you, Tank didn't attack the commissioner. That's completely insane! But for some reason, he was here, and if we want to figure out why and find him ourselves, we're going to need the police department's help. Frank is our best option."

"They're going to protect their own, Larry," said Dawn. "They're going to go after him, with lethal force if need be. Can't you see that?"

"You have a better idea for finding him?" said Larry. "Lexie, you want to go back to the house and concoct another potion? Personally I think it's a little late for that."

I didn't know what to say. "I..."

Dawn snorted and threw up her hands. She turned her back on us and waltzed off.

I watched her walk away. "Way to go. You've been out of the basement for less than an hour, and already you're back to being an asshole."

"Me?" Larry's eyes widened in shock. "You asked me to help find Tank. This is how I can help. Whatever beef Frank might've had with him, he won't have one with me. Promise."

"*Stuttgart!*"

We turned to find Frank Connors storming across the night shadowed street. Anger twisted his face, and I could practically smell the smoke coming from his ears.

"Frank," said Larry in relief. "I kept telling these flunkies that—"

Frank pushed the barricade to the side as he barged his way through. "Don't say a thing. Don't say a *god-damned word.*" He pushed into Larry's face and jabbed a finger in his chest. "What do you think this is? *A game?* I..."

Suddenly, Connors coughed. He retched a little as he took a step back from Larry, his eyes narrowing in a mixture of confusion and disgust. "Larry... What the hell happened to you? Is this why you've been MIA for weeks?"

"It's a long story," he said. "I don't want to get into it."

"You don't want to...?" Connors' brows drew back together,

and fire glinted in his eyes. "Fine. It doesn't matter. What matters is we're done. Finished. I told her this morning." He jabbed another angry finger in my direction. "I told her if he so much as breathed on the wrong person, we'd take action. And instead he tries to *murder the commsissioner!*"

"Whoa," said Larry. "Slow down, man. You're not making any sense. Tank wouldn't have any reason to—"

Connors slammed Larry in the chest with both of his palms. "To what? *To kill?* Guess what, Larry? You don't know him anymore. None of you do, but I got a good look at him this morning when you bailed him out. I saw a broken man, one who'd lost all hope. And instead of getting him some help, what? You take him on a mission where he goes insane with bloodlust?"

"That's not true," I said. "We made a breakthrough. He was getting better. He wanted to help."

Connors stared icicles at me. "It doesn't matter what he wanted. You should've known better. This is on your head as much as his. I should arrest you for gross negligence."

"Look, I wasn't at the gala," said Larry. "I can't speak to what happened there, but *this?* This isn't Tank. You say he attacked the commissioner? He's not a deranged killer. You know that. He wouldn't do this without a reason."

Connors practically shook with rage. "All I know is I have a half-dozen witnesses who saw a Kodiak bear barge into the commish's house and nearly take his head off. And beyond witnesses, the chief has a very good security system. I've seen the video. It's Tank. Why did he do it? Beats the hell out of me. Maybe he wasn't a deranged killer before, but loss can do some fucked up things to a man. Maybe he blames us for not stopping Benedict before he killed his ex-wife. Maybe he's got a death wish and he thinks this is the easiest way out. Frankly, I don't know, and I don't care. But hear me carefully. Your association with him, your friendship? It means *nothing*. We *will* find him, and we *will* put him down, by any means necessary."

A lump sat in my throat, and my gut roiled with tension. Based on the way Larry croaked, the tirade has impacted him, too. "Frank. After all we've been through..."

The detective cut him off with a murderous glare. "You better pray you find him before we do, because he's not likely to make it out of a confrontation with us alive. And if you *do* find him, get him locked up behind bars immediately. The APD doesn't deal leniently with people who harbor fugitives."

Connors turned and stormed off. The air crackled in his wake, and not purely metaphorically. There was an extra sizzle there, a lingering ripple of magical energy in the air. I didn't think the detective had any magical powers, but perhaps his anger had been enough to tap into the forces around him and I was finally attuned enough to realize it.

Larry hung his head and pressed a hand to his forehead. "Shit..."

He looked about how I felt. "I tried to tell you."

Larry sighed. "You did, and I didn't listen. Rubbing it in won't help, though."

I don't think he intended for his remark to cut me, but it did. The part of me that liked getting in fights wanted to say something, but I knew better. "Come on. Let's get out of here before the officer with the gut and the tazer fetish comes back."

As we walked toward the Suburban, Larry's and my isolation struck me. "Hey... Where's Dawn?"

Larry looked around before nodding toward the truck. "A few steps ahead of us, I guess."

Dawn leaned against the Suburban's hatch, back toward us. "Time to go, Dawn. This is a dead end."

"Way ahead of you." Something crackled as she spoke, and I heard voices.

"What the...?" I turned the corner and found Dawn cradling a black plastic rectangle in her hands. More voices sparked from the speaker unit amid a cloud of static. "A walkie-talkie? Where you'd get that?"

Dawn waved a hand at me. "I swiped it from one of the officers while you two distracted them by fighting with Frank. Pipe down. I think I've found them."

"Found who?" said Larry.

"BSI. Their comm channel. Who else?"

The speaker crackled again. This time the voices were distinct. "Gamma team, do you copy? Can you assist? Over."

"Gamma team?" said Larry.

Dawn jammed a finger against her lips. "Don't give away the game plan." She pressed the button on the side and spoke into the receiver. "Gamma team. Can you repeat? Over."

"How long have you been doing this?" I asked. "What if they realize you're not who they think you are?"

Dawn glared at me as the walkie-talkie crackled again. "I said, target spotted at the Texas capitol building. Calling all nearby teams. Can you assist? Over."

"Copy that. On our way." Dawn hopped to it and pulled open the rear driver's side door. She paused to look at Larry and me, both of whom stood frozen to the asphalt.

"Well, what are you waiting for?" she said. "You don't think BSI has some *other* target they're sending teams to neutralize, do you? Come on! Let's go!"

26

I GUNNED THE ENGINE AS I HEADED OVER THE WEST 15TH Street bridge. In the last five minutes, I'd stopped asking myself why. Why Tank had lost it at the Arbor Crest Country Club, why he'd attacked the city's police chief, and why he'd seemingly shifted his focus to something at the state capitol. I'd stopped asking myself those questions because neither I nor Larry nor Dawn had any answers. None of the attacks made sense, but unlike Frank Connors, I *did* believe in Tank. I knew he wasn't crazy. I knew he wasn't a deranged sociopath or a violent murderer, which meant it stood to reason there was something driving him along his current destructive path. We just had to figure out what it was.

Answers would have to wait, though. For the time being, saving Tank from the police and BSI was our only priority.

"We're going to need a plan," I said.

"You think?" said Larry. "Of course we need a plan. Kind of hard to put one together when we have no idea what we're running into, though."

Dawn grunted from the back seat. "I think it's safe to

assume we'll find Tank, he'll still be pissed off, and a bunch of BSI thugs are going to be trying to shoot him."

"Still not specific enough for us to put together an extraction plan," said Larry.

I ran through a light that lingered on yellow longer than it should've. Maybe I was just going that fast. "When I faced off with him at the country club, he attacked me. Lunged right at me. I tried to hit him with a fire spell, but it bounced off him."

"Because he's a werebear," said Larry. "He's tough as nails, especially when he's in bear form. What did you expect?"

I glanced at the street signs, most of which were cast in shadow and hard to read. "My point is if we need to immobilize him, we should consider something other than magic."

"Or we use the right *kind* of magic," said Larry. "No offense, but attacking a bear with fire is dumb. Even setting a normal bear on fire is a terrible idea."

Where did I need to turn? Lavaca? No. That was one way. Guadalupe then. I was halfway past it before I realized it.

The truck shuddered as I pumped the brakes and cranked on the wheel. "I take it you have a better idea?"

"Stasis." Larry clung to the door handle built into the upholstery. "It worked when I hit him in the head during that vampire rave. I'll just cast a stasis spell on his whole body."

"And then what?" said Dawn. "We drag his unresponsive, fifteen hundred pound carcass off and stuff it in the car? Have you been hitting the weights while you've been hiding in the basement, Larry?"

"I'll use a levitation spell," he said. "Doesn't matter how heavy he is."

"You sure you can do all that?" I asked. "You said your magic isn't what it used to be."

Larry growled. "Hey, you want to help? I won't say no. But let's worry about the magic later and find Tank first."

I slowed as I spotted the capitol's dome over the tips of nearby buildings, the Goddess of Liberty and her five pointed star of Texas clearly in hand. The bright lights that shot up the building's sides made the structure look more gray than the true pale pink of the red granite that comprised it.

The streets were practically empty because of the hour, which meant I didn't have to worry about cross traffic, but figuring out how to get close to the building was another story. "Crap. Should I go down to 11th? Where do I park?"

"Do you think anyone cares at this hour?" said Larry. "Get as close as you can."

I hooked a left on 12th. That turned out to be the right choice. I screeched to a halt at the foot of a gate to one of the driveways that curved off between trees to the capitol itself.

I put the car in park. Larry looked at me like I'd lost my mind. "What are you doing?"

"Parking? What does it look like I'm doing?"

Larry pointed at the gate. "Not here. Get us close. Go!"

"Larry, I'm not—"

"Frank already hates us. How much worse is it going to get?" Larry flicked a hand at the gate, and it burst inward as if blasted by a couple ounces of C4. So much for his magic not working.

I hit the gas again and pulled up to the building proper. I'd been there a long time ago as part of a school field trip, but I'd forgotten just how large the thing was. The main portion of the capitol was four stories high, but the dome stretched at least that much higher above it. Thankfully, congress didn't appear to be in session at one thirty in the morning, nor was there a police force already on site, but a couple of black BSI Escalades were parked outside the front doors.

I screeched to a halt behind them. "Crap. They're already here."

Dawn's walkie-talkie crackled, and the same voice from earlier sprouted from the speaker. Static caused the voice to cut in and out, making it difficult to tell what he was saying. "—third floor—*crackle*—got eyes on—*crackle*—move up one. Careful now."

"Did you catch that?" I asked.

"Sounds like Tank is in there," said Dawn. "What the hell is he doing *in* the capitol?"

"We'll ask him once we have him back at the house," said Larry. "Come on."

We piled out and ran to the doors, which hung loose on their hinges. The wood around the locks had been smashed as if hit with a battering ram.

Larry pulled the nearest one open and we surged inside, skidding to a halt as we reached the tile rotunda featuring the seals of the six sovereign nations that had ruled Texas, past and present. Shouts sounded from the upper levels, as did a roar that echoed along the limestone.

Larry cocked his head. "He's above us. Third floor, maybe. BSI has to be close."

I sniffed the air with my magical sense. "No. He's higher. I think he's in the top dome."

"What makes you say that?" said Larry.

"My Smell," I said. "It hasn't gone away after I quaffed the potion. There's a magical signature up there. It's big, and it feels... off somehow. Angry, obviously, but there's something else strange about it, too." I sniffed again, and then I detected it.

Licorice. God-damnit. Why was that scent back? It didn't make any sense.

Larry nodded, taking my word as gospel. "The top dome is restricted, but I know how to get there. I did a job here once that required me to climb to the top of the spire."

"You did?" said Dawn. "What kind of job?"

"The kind that makes me hope nobody ever pulls up the floor underneath the Lieutenant Governor's office. Come on."

Larry led us out of the rotunda, into an adjoining hallway, and up a staircase held up by grooved white columns. I heard thumps and shouts in the distance, as well as another of Tank's roars. Thankfully, I didn't pick up on any gunshots or cries of pain.

Up and around the curved staircase we ran, taking the steps two and three at a time. On the third floor, I spotted a flash of black, the blur of a BSI operative darting between hallways, but I don't think they spotted me and I doubt they heard us among the commotion. Dawn's walkie talkie crackled and more fragmented sentences spewed out, something about him getting away and calling in the big guns.

Once we reached the top public level, Larry led us to the railing overlooking the rotunda, then into a back hallway. He darted toward a much smaller staircase, one barricaded by a velvet rope that hung between brass posts. I'd never seen much athleticism out of the guy, but he leapfrogged the rope without catching his feet, and on we went. Up the stairs, now in single file. Our footsteps clattered off the tile before echoing off the stone walls. Somewhere above us, I heard more thumps. I thought it might be Tank's footsteps, but they were rhythmic. Choppy. The thumping of blades, over and over. A helicopter?

"Guys, I think the police are closing in," I said. "We need to move fast."

"Moving as fast as I can under the circumstances," said Larry.

We burst onto the top level of the main dome and screeched to a halt beside the railing. On the other side, Tank lumbered along the pink tile. Part of me was awed. It truly was a grand space, with an open column in the center that stretched as far down to the floor as up to the top spire. I felt as if I'd gotten separated from my class and would get reprimanded by the principal for wandering off, but even the architectural majesty couldn't distract me from the sight of Tank.

Something was wrong with him. The fur along the ridge of his back stood on end, like a dog with its hackles up, and his eyes had turned into yawning pools of darkness. When he stared at us, it was without an ounce of compassion—or familiarity.

Shouts sounded from the stairs. Larry waved a hand at the mouth of the steps. "Lexie. Block it off. Quick."

I didn't think he meant by shoving a bench into it. I grabbed ahold of the magical energies around me and cast a quick ward across the exit, hoping it would hold the folks from BSI. As I did so, the thumping of the helicopter got louder. I peered out the windows, but I couldn't see it. I'd half expected spotlights to dance across the exterior of the dome and for a voice amplified via megaphone to instruct us to come out with our hands up.

Larry took a few cautious steps forward, his hands extended. "Hey there, Tank. It's me. I'm sorry I wasn't there to help you with what you've been going through. I've been swimming through a swamp of suck myself these last couple weeks. It's going to be okay, though. You've just got to come with us. Help us out."

For a moment, Tank hunched there on all fours, staring at us, and I thought he'd gotten through to him. Then he reared and unleashed the loudest, most full-throated roar I'd ever heard. It shook the windows and drowned the sound of the helicopter circling overhead. Then he slammed his paws on the floor, cracking the tiles underneath. He glared at us and bared his teeth in aggression.

"Well, I had to try. Sorry about this, big guy, but you leave me no choice." Larry lifted his arms. I felt a chill as he sucked energy from the air around us. A bubble devoid of time that smelled of fresh spring shoots and rotting leaves coalesced in front of me. It flew across the empty space, a ripple of air and magic that slammed into Tank.

I thought it might send him flying. Larry probably expected it to freeze him in place, given that it was a stasis spell and all.

Instead, it did jack shit.

Larry's jaw dropped. "That's bad."

Tank roared again, and he took off around the balcony toward us.

27

I GATHERED MY MAGIC AND PREPARED TO CAST SOMETHING —anything, maybe another ward of protection to keep Tank from tearing us limb from limb—but I didn't get the opportunity. Glass shattered as six windows imploded simultaneously. Black boots flew in first, followed by the bodies they belonged too. Soldiers clad in tactical vests, cargo pants, long sleeve black shirts, and helmets with tinted visors. They released their rappel lines as they rolled across the floor, shards of glass crunching underneath them. I wasn't sure if they were police or BSI, but as they ripped submachine guns from their belts and trained them on Tank, I realized it didn't matter. Their intent was clear enough.

One of the commandos yelled. "Open fire!"

Machine guns crackled and spat as bullets flew. Tank roared as lead missiles bounced off his thick hide. He broke into a run, slamming the nearest SWAT member with a paw the size of a frying pan. The guy went flying. His back popped as he smashed into a pillar. A spiderweb of cracks spread out behind him on the limestone as Tank continued his charge. Bullets pinged as they ricocheted off him and then the floor, the melody mingling with the tinkle of bullet casings bouncing along the tile. He smashed another commando, who screamed as he fell over the railing and fell four stories to the floor.

Tank was twenty feet away now and closing. Larry stepped in front of us, his hand held out as if protecting a child in the front seat of a car. "Get back!" he shouted to us. "Now!"

Dawn dove for cover, which would've been the smart thing to do, but I'd just seen Larry's stasis spell fail to even daze Tank. I remembered how he'd uncorked on me in the golf club, and I wasn't about to let him blast Larry with something as powerful when the guy clearly didn't have his full arsenal to protect himself. I dove forward, summoning the most powerful ward I could before throwing it in front of us.

In one sense, it worked. Tank lunged and swiped at us with his paw, but the magical shield dissipated the energy of his blow over a space of about a meter and a half. The problem was that Larry and I were right behind it. The blow lifted us off our feet, almost gently, but it nonetheless sent us flying. I braced myself for another back-breaking limestone punch, but instead I felt shards of glass ripping at my clothes as I flew out one of the already broken windows into the night sky. A rappel cord whipped around me. I grasped at it desperately, trying to grab it with one hand and hold onto Larry with the other, but I was moving too fast. The cord slipped and burned my palm as I tried to grip it, and Larry's weight pulled on my arm, dragging me down.

My grip gave and I fell. I screamed, but the sudden appearance of a tarnished copper roof turned the yell into a yelp. I slammed on the metal with a clang, the breath vanishing from my lungs as if beaten out of me. Larry groaned as he landed simultaneously, the sound muffled by the mechanized thump of helicopter blades buzzing overhead. I wheezed as I turned onto my back, lifting an arm to shield my eyes from the rush of air. The helicopter dipped down low, maybe twenty feet from the edge of the top dome. A few flashlights cut the night sky from its open hatch, with more commandos in black leaning from it. The words BSI were pained on the side in white.

I wanted to curse, but I still couldn't breathe. I tried to push myself up, but as I did so I realized I was sliding. The helicopter above drifted away from me, or rather I from it based on its position relative to the dome. I glanced at my feet and spotted a yawning abyss as I reached the edge of the four and a half story drop in front of me.

I reached for my magic as the darkness grew, trying to think. I knew how to cast wards, glyphs, summon ice and fire, but I'd never learned to fly. My hands and feet scrabbled at the slick metal around me, trying to find purchase, but there was none. My heart leapt into my throat and cold fear gripped me.

"Lexie!" Larry shouted at my back, and I heard a thump. As my feet dipped over the edge, Larry slid alongside me, grabbing me around the arm. His shoes squeaked as his soles left rubber smears along the roof. "Hang on!"

I squeezed tight, but momentum is a bitch. I felt a jolt and my grip held, but Larry's shoes didn't. He grunted. I squawked. He tipped forward, and we both went over the edge.

This time I didn't bother grasping at the magic. The panic had full hold of me, and I simply screamed.

Thank God Larry had fifteen years of experience on me.

He mumbled something in Latin and our descent slowed. The wind in my ears went from a whistle to a whisper, but we didn't stop entirely. The ground approached more quickly than

I would've liked, but at least I didn't slam face first into the dirt. I decelerated and bounced about three feet, as if I'd secretly been squirreled away in one of those giant inflatable hamster balls. I bounced a few more times before rolling to a stop in the grass.

I groaned as I rolled to my knees. "What the heck kind of spell was that?"

"Part levitation, part protection ward." Larry lay on his back, breathing heavily. "Best I could whip up in short notice."

I was just glad it had worked. Best not to mention that part though. "You'll have to teach me."

He nodded as a resounding crash like that of a boulder being cleaved in twain split the air. I looked up toward the dome, but the rest of the state house blocked my view. "Jesus. Dawn's still up there."

Larry wheezed as he stumbled to his knees. "I'm not sure she's the one we should be worried about. She has a knack for slipping out of tight situations. Tank, on the other hand..."

Bits of rubble tumbled over the side of the capitol. The bounce following our landing had tossed me out of the radius of destruction, but I nonetheless pushed myself to my feet and ran into the street. From there, I had a good enough vantage to see what had transpired above. As I'd half expected based on the shower of debris and the loud crack, something had punched a hole in the side of the dome—or should I say, *someone*.

Tank clung to the exterior like a shrunk down version of King Kong, punching handholds into the stone as he clawed his way up. Flashlights trailed him from the walkway below, and cracks of gunfire still filled the air. Not all of it was coming from the building. The helicopter had closed in, now hovering a bare fifteen feet away from him. Commandos in the open door fired rifles, their muzzles flashing.

"Christ," I said. "When did Tank get so nimble?"

Apparently I spoke too soon. Another of the BSI goons appeared in the open hatch holding something long and bulky. From so far away I couldn't tell if it was a gas grenade launcher or an RPG or something else entirely, but whatever it was, Tank didn't like it. I heard his roar over the thump of the chopper blades.

And then he leapt.

Through the air. Fifteen feet at least, action movie style, reaching toward the helicopter with his massive outstretched paws.

The pilot was quick on the draw. The helicopter banked, but not quickly enough. Tank wrapped a lone paw around one of the chopper's landing skids. The whole vehicle spun and tilted as Tank's weight threw the balance completely off.

"Holy. Crap." Larry stared at the ordeal with his mouth open. I'd probably catch flies myself if I didn't stop gaping.

Tank swiped at the helicopter, but he couldn't get his second paw on the skid. The chopper continued to spin, but apparently the pilot had a plan in place for the rare event that a Kodiak werebear managed to grab partially but not completely ahold of his flying aircraft, because as soon as he got the spinning under control he tilted the helicopter to the south and hit the throttle.

Larry grabbed me by the arm. "What are you waiting for? Time to go!"

I looked at him like he was crazy. "You want me to follow a *helicopter?* I know the Suburban flew once, but I don't have any fairy dust on me."

As the chopper's roar faded, a new sound grew to replace it. The sound of sirens. Lots of them.

"We need to save Tank," said Larry. "And helping him isn't the only reason we need to make ourselves scarce."

He was right of course. "What about Dawn?"

"I told you, she's great at not dying. *Come on!*"

We ran back to the truck. The engine roared and I slammed the shift into drive. The Suburban lurched as I hit the gas, tires squealing as I pulled it around and sped down the drive. The back of the car fishtailed as I wove through the entry gates, up the slight incline, and onto Guadalupe. I spotted red and blue flashing lights out of the corners of my vision, but I didn't let off the gas. "Do you have eyes on the chopper?"

"They're heading south, toward the river. Can't you go any faster?"

I glanced at the speedometer. It hadn't even hit sixty. "Not without help. Remember that time you magically supercharged this sucker?"

Larry nodded. His eyes shifted to the truck's hood. His eyelids narrowed, and suddenly the 'burban roared. I think the front wheels lifted off the pavement for a fraction of a second, but when they landed the truck took off like a roller coaster. The acceleration pushed me into my seat, and the police sirens even changed pitch.

As the truck peaked at about ninety, Larry leaned forward, looking through the windshield. "I see them. They're headed toward the river, but we're closing in."

"I'll take the first street bridge." I avoided the South Congress bridge if at all possible. The city still hadn't fixed the pothole left by Ivan Romanov's spontaneous combustion.

"Wait a sec." Larry leaned further forward. "Is that...?"

I blasted through a red light at top speed. "Is that what?"

"It is. Another helicopter. BSI has *two* helicopters? Why in the world do these guys need our business?"

I heard the thrum of the blades as it passed over us, then spotted the cones of light beaming from the helicopter as it sped south after the first. Even in the night sky, the bright headlights were enough to illuminate a gleaming metal cylinder that hung from underneath the thing's nose.

"Christ almighty," I said. "Is that a minigun?"

"Thirty millimeter auto cannon, probably," said Larry. "I didn't think those were legal."

I mashed on the brakes as the shimmer of the Colorado River appeared past the West Cesar Chavez stoplight. I hadn't intended to bring the truck to a standstill, but as I once again spotted the chopper from which Tank hung, I couldn't help but stop and stare.

Tank had managed to pull himself up. The helicopter spun out of control as Tank's furry behind hung out one side of the hatch. Someone jumped from the opposite side, then another. Two parachutes opened in quick succession. The helicopter dipped precipitously to one side as it spun, and it started to veer toward the water.

My voice was a whisper in my ears. "Oh, no."

A loud hammer of gunfire caused me to jump in my seat. The second BSI copter's cannon roared, the muzzle flashing as yellow-orange streaks cut across the night sky like meteorites. Sparks erupted from the fishtailing helicopter. It might've been my imagination, but I thought I heard metal tearing and saw blood splatter as bullets made contact with Tank's thick hide.

The helicopter pitched even further to the side. As it did so, a cloud of flame erupted from it with an ear-splitting blast. The tail boom whipped up, and the entire chopper flipped upside down before plunging two hundred feet into the Colorado River. Water splashed high in an angry geyser. Only then did I realize I was shouting. "Tank! *NOOOOO!!*"

The second helicopter's lights played over the water's rippling surface, dark and choppy. A bit of gasoline burned across the surface, but it spent itself quickly, leaving nothing but frothy black death rippling across the waves.

We should've left. BSI's attack helicopter certainly did, but Larry and I stayed, despite his protests.

I had to watch for bubbles.

I didn't find any.

28

I SAT ON THE COUCH IN FRONT OF OUR TV. I DIDN'T KNOW what time it was, nor did I care. I'd barely slept since driving back to the house with Larry, but I didn't feel tired. I didn't feel hungry either, though a voice in the recesses of my mind told me I should eat. All I felt was despair.

I guess it was better than not feeling anything at all.

A talking head on the TV blathered on about the attack. The official story was that a right-wing militia had invaded the capitol overnight and threatened to squat there until Texas invoked its constitutional right to secede from the Union, as stipulated by the Congressional Joint Resolution for Annexation of Texas to the United States of 1845, which as other pundits were quick to point out didn't actually guarantee any such thing. Supposedly, the militia in question was headed by former pro-wrestler Jason "The Savage Beast" Mendoza, who was about six-foot nine, three hundred and fifty pounds, sported wild hair and a chest length beard, and apparently must've been wearing a Bigfoot costume for anyone to have believed he could've passed as a Kodiak bear. Then again, all the eye witnesses the news folks had rustled up had seen the event unfold from a distance, and the videos they'd captured on their phones were blurry and didn't prove much of anything either way. In the official version, though, the helicopter had been owned and operated by the Texas State Guard, and no chopper had exploded and fallen into the Colorado River. That, instead, had been the byproduct of a faulty motor on a passing boat that had caught fire.

None of it made any sense, but it didn't have to. People would buy it. And none of it would change the fact that Tank was gone.

I'd held out hope at first. Tank was tough. If he could survive .22s and 9 millimeters and .45 caliber rounds, then why not big ass armor-piercing rounds from a chain gun? Why couldn't he survive a violent gasoline explosion and the heat and high speed shrapnel that it launched everywhere with deadly indiscretion? Why couldn't he survive the two hundred foot fall into a watery death trap while encased in the twisted metal tomb of a former helicopter?

But that was the rub, really. Because while I had a sliver of faith that Tank might've survived the mayhem he succumbed to in the skies, I knew for a fact he couldn't breathe underwater. And he never came out.

I knew that beyond what my own eyes told me. Despite our fight with him earlier in the night, Larry was eventually able to get Frank on the phone. Because he'd gone on a violent rampage, attacked the police commissioner, and bashed up the state capitol, Connors had been unsurprisingly reticent to take our word on Tank's demise, so he'd ordered officers to patrol the edges of the Colorado river for several miles downstream from the 1st Street bridge.

Nobody came ashore.

They'd send the divers in later to recover the wreck, but it would probably take a while. They'd try to keep things quiet, as random speedboats that went kerplunk in the night didn't warrant sending in coroner dive teams.

Not that I needed to see Tank's bloated corpse to believe he was gone. Unlike some of the other male members of the house, I dealt with grief in a pretty logical manner. Once he hadn't come up, I'd moved from denial right into anger.

And despite the grief that enveloped me, I was still pretty damn pissed off. I was pissed at BSI for bringing military grade gear into a fight against one of my best friends, a fight I was pretty sure they instigated, even if I couldn't prove it. I was furious at the police, not only because they were as eager to dispatch Tank as BSI but because they wouldn't prosecute BSI for his murder. Frank made that crystal clear on his phone call. As far as they were concerned, Tank got what was coming to him, and if it had been police SWAT members in the place of private BSI ones, they probably would've acted the same way. Finally, I was furious with myself.

Because I knew I'd let Tank down. I could've saved him. If only we'd gotten through to him earlier.

The couch shook, and I looked up. Larry had sat down opposite me, his eyes focused on the TV. I hadn't heard him walk up, nor smelled him for that matter. Then again, I don't think I'd processed anything the anchormen and women on the newscast had said for the last ten minutes. My attention had been focused on the past, not the present.

Larry didn't say anything. He watched the television with a creased brow and dull eyes, occasionally exhaling forcefully with a sigh. He didn't need to breathe now that he was dead, so the action must've been purposeful.

After a minute or two, I broke the silence. "How's Dawn?"

He shrugged. "Same as the rest of us. Tired. Angry. Sad. A little broken inside."

"Do you think she wants company?"

Larry shook his head. "Not yet. Maybe later."

I turned back to the newscast. They were showing a live bird's eye view of the destruction of the capitol. Tank had done a number on the place. How could people believe a former pro-wrestler turned militia leader could've done that?

"This isn't your fault, Lexie."

I turned back to face him. "Are you talking about Tank's death?"

"Of course. What else would I be talking about?"

"What makes you think I blame myself for what happened to him?"

Larry lifted an eyebrow. "I know how you think. I know how you internalize grief, in part because I've already died once and helped walk you through it."

I hated the fact that he was right, even if he had dropped by to lend emotional support. "I don't blame myself."

"You don't entirely blame yourself, you mean."

"That's right. You're much more at fault than I am."

Larry snorted. "There we go."

"You weren't there for him when he needed you. You could've come up from your bunker. Helped him through it. Both of you were dealing with the same sort of grief, the same acceptance of death, him of his ex-wife's and you of your own. You could've held his hand as he cried and vice versa."

"Metaphorically, I assume."

"Damnit, Larry. Admit it. You had a role in this. His blood is on your hands, too. Maybe not much, but a little."

"Of course it is."

I hadn't expected him to agree with me. I blinked, shocked.

"It's on my hands to the same degree it's on yours, or Dawn's. It's on BSI's hands and Frank Connors'. We all played a role. But you can't act as if Tank didn't play the greatest role in this himself. He made choices. Bad ones, that all of us could've helped steer him away from, but he could've taken a different path. It was up to him."

I shook my head, still angry. "I disagree. I mean, yes, you're right, but at the same time, none of this makes any sense. This time yesterday morning he'd been lying at the bottom of a cell, still drunk, when Dawn and I bailed him out. We talked to him, broke through to him, or at least Dawn did. He realized where he'd screwed up, where'd he'd fallen off the tracks. I saw him make the decision to do better, Larry. I saw it in his eyes, and yet roughly twelve hours later he goes nuts, turns, attacks a bunch of people, and sets off on a murderous rampage? It's insane! He was depressed, not suicidal."

Larry shook his head. "I don't know what to tell you. Maybe he was putting on a brave face to keep you and Dawn from worrying. Maybe you read him wrong."

"He came with me on a job afterwards. Of his own volition! I told him to stay and rest, but he came with me because he wanted to right a wrong. Did I read that incorrectly, too?"

Larry shared an empathetic glance. "People grieve in different ways, Lexie. They go through highs and lows. They have breakthroughs and setbacks. Could've been he'd almost gotten to the acceptance stage and something happened, something triggered him and he fell back into anger. You get a were-bear angry and all bets are off."

"But what?" I said. "What could've set him off? We were providing security at a gala, for Christ's sake. Unless one of those BSI assholes came after him directly, I don't see why he would've gone off the deep end."

"I don't either," said Larry. "But rest assured if they *did* do it, they're going to pay. Dearly."

The phone rang, and Bill answered. "You've reached the Nyte Patrol. How can I help you?"

Bill had been practically silent since we got back. I don't think he and Tank had ever been that close, but Bill was none-theless angry we hadn't taken him with us, either to the gala or on our hunt to find Tank. Really, I think his mood was just an expression of grief at Tank's loss.

"I'm sorry, ma'am," said Bill. "We're not taking new clients right now. We're dealing with extenuating circumstances. ... Well, look, that sounds like a new job to me. ... Yes, you may be a former client, but... Okay. One moment please."

Bill's voice got louder as he projected out of his jar. "Lexie? Can you take this?"

I turned from the couch, staring toward Bill's table. "Who is it?"

"It's that lady from Nine Moons," said Bill. "Augusta Shade. Apparently that job of hers isn't over after all."

29

I CONSIDERED TELLING BILL TO HANG UP ON HER AND BE done with it, but I nonetheless got to my feet and lumbered over to Larry's desk. I picked the receiver off the console and held it to my ear. "Lexie Rodriguez speaking."

"Lexie. This is Augusta Shade. With Nine Moons?"

"Yes, Ms. Shade. Bill told me. What seems to be the problem?"

"The problem is that duende who broke into my store came back last night, and it made an even bigger mess than it did the first time! My herb section in back looks like a tornado blew through it. I have at least two dozen powdered potion ingredients that were thrown to the ground and trampled, and I'm pretty sure it broke into my staff refrigerator and drank all the milk."

It took effort to remain polite, which was something I needed practice with. "I'm sorry to hear that, but I don't see how this is my concern. If you'll recall, we didn't solve your break-in problem. Perhaps you should contact BSI."

Augusta sighed. "That's the thing. I *did* call them.

Multiple times, but they won't give me the time of day. They claim they captured the duende and relocated it and that if I've suffered another intrusion, then it must be at the hands of a different culprit who isn't covered by their initial agreement."

"So hire them again to look into the new instance for you."

"I wouldn't do such a thing, not when it's clear they didn't solve my problem to begin with, which is what I paid them for. But even if I wanted to hire them again, they wouldn't let me. The representative on the phone told me they simply weren't interested in cases of my *magnitude*—her word—and she suggested I try a less in demand business."

"Which is why you called us."

"Yes. I mean, no. Look, you were already here. You looked into my case. At the very least, come take another gander. Tell me if the individual who broke into my store is the same one who was here a few days ago. That at least will give me evidence to take back to BSI and tell them they're in breach of contract."

Augusta wouldn't have asked us to come if she'd had any idea of the hell I'd been through over the last twelve hours, so I had to assume she was clueless when it came to current events. "Ms. Shade, I've had a very long day. I've suffered in ways you couldn't possibly imagine. I'm sorry, but—"

"Please," she said. "I'll pay you handsomely. Both for the new work and the work you already did. I want to get this resolved, and I need help from someone who knows what they're doing and cares about their clients."

Maybe she thought the subtle dig at BSI would sway my opinion. Maybe she was right. "I'll keep that in mind. Goodbye, Ms. Shade."

I hung up the phone. Bill lifted an eyebrow at me in curiosity, but I shook my head and walked back to the couch.

I sat down and stared at the television in silence. After a minute, it was Larry who broke the silence this time. "Care to tell me what that was about?"

"It was the owner of Nine Moons. I can't remember if I told you about that case or not. A duende broke into her shop and made a mess of the back room. BSI caught it and released it who knows where. Apparently it found its way back. Or not. I don't know. Could've been another one."

"Hold on. A *duende?*" Larry leaned forward, suddenly engaged.

"Yeah. Why is that a big deal?"

"Well, because no one's seen one in Texas in... I don't know. Ever? Even in the parts of the world in which they live, they're super hard to find. They're incredibly reclusive. I'm surprised one of them would've risked breaking into someone's store even if they were living around here."

I didn't know what to say, so I shrugged.

"Did you get a look at it?" asked Larry.

I shook my head. "BSI carted it off in the middle of the night. Why are you so into this? Do you have a secret love of zoology you've never told me about?"

"Duende are sentient creatures, as far as I'm aware. You don't study them in supernatural zoology courses, but... whatever. That's not the point. I don't know. It's strange, is all."

We sat in silence for few seconds. Despite our loss, I felt a smile creeping on. "You're regretting hiding out in the basement for the last two weeks. You *miss* this, don't you?"

Larry suddenly wouldn't make eye contact. "I mean... looking for cures for zombieism isn't the most engaging thing in the world, especially when you're not making any progress. I've never claimed I didn't like this job. It's been my professional focus for over a decade."

And lord knows he didn't have much of a personal life. "Look, Larry. I don't want to take a new job right now. Not with everything that's happened. I can't. I'm in no state to work."

"No. Of course not. It's not the right time. Our place is here. Making sure we don't let what happened to Tank happen to the rest of us. There will be time to sort out the business end of things later."

Larry wasn't very good at keeping the disappointment out of his voice. Maybe he was just curious, or maybe he was the type to distract himself from his emotional problems with work. Now that I thought about it, I was almost sure the latter was true.

"Of course," I said. "This isn't really a new job. It's an extension of an existing job. We never solved Augusta's problem."

Larry's eyebrows drew together. "So what you're saying is, it's our professional responsibility to see it through."

"I suppose it is. But just this one case. For now."

Larry nodded slowly. "Right. For now."

30

THE DOOR CHIME RANG AS I PUSHED MY WAY INTO NINE Moons. Augusta stood at the counter, today wearing a simple white dress with a colorful floral print that flared at the hips. She kept her hair tied with the same patterned black and yellow headband, though. It must've been her favorite.

The woman relaxed as she caught sight of us. "Oh, thank goodness. I wasn't sure if you'd come."

I stepped to the counter. "To be honest, I wasn't sure if we should. You should've been upfront with us that you'd hired BSI to investigate the case, and you should've given us compensation for the work we performed. Although if we're being honest, I guess we should've had you sign a contract from the get go. That's on us. To be frank, we need to reevaluate some of our business practices."

Augusta's nose wrinkled as she glanced at Larry, but to her credit she didn't mention his aroma. "No, you're right. It's my fault more than yours. I shouldn't have put you in that position, but I'm going to make things right. I'll pay you for the time you've spent on the case, plus whatever else you need. Fees, overhead, you name it. I just really need your help. I can't keep having creatures breaking into my store and ruining my inventory. Insurance won't cover magical supplies, and I'm losing money every time something gets destroyed. Please. BSI won't even return my calls. You're the best option I have left."

The mention of BSI sent the hairs on the back of my neck standing up. I'd be happy if I never heard or interacted with those ruthless thugs ever again.

I glanced at Larry. "What do you think?"

He tried to play it casual, but I know he was piqued by the prospect of finding a duende. "I've been called worse by clients. You want to show us the scene of the crime, Ms. Shade?"

She nodded. "Yes. Please. Come with me."

Augusta led us through the tight aisles before unlocking the Employees Only door and ushering us into the back.

I immediately noticed what she meant. Several of her shelves had been knocked over, the contents strewn across the floor. Powders of various colors mingled with crushed rocks, feathers, and dried mushrooms underneath them. The carefully tended plants that had sprouted from racks in the center of the room were even more of a disaster, half of them upturned, the other half shredded, with leaves and stems and shoots fifteen feet away in the aisles and atop the wares. Perhaps even more importantly, however, was the scent that lingered over everything.

As I opened myself to the magical energies around me, I sniffed it out right away. That damn licorice Smell. It was everywhere. Over the mixed powders and potion components, slicking the leaves and grasses scattered across the tile, up and down each of the aisles. The place stank of it. Considering it had been days since I'd quaffed the potion, that either meant I was improving in how to detect Smells faster than I'd ever expected I would, or the creature who'd left the aroma had rubbed its metaphorical scent glands over everything real good.

Augusta waved toward the carnage as she led us to the center of the wrecked garden. "Do you see what I mean? I don't know what I did to piss this duende off, but it's ruined my herbs! There are thousands of dollars worth of damage to my plants alone. Maybe it's angry it got caught, but why come back? Why tear up my shop? Shouldn't its beef be with BSI? And honestly, did they release the dang thing back into the woods? Shouldn't a creature this destructive be put down, or carted into a national park at least?"

Larry's brow furrowed. He glanced around the store, not just at the displays that had been knocked over. He glanced at the ceiling, the walls, the doors. He gave Augusta a nod. "If you don't mind my asking, since I wasn't here before, what happened during the first break-in? What did the intruder go after?"

"The plants mostly," said Augusta. "The masterwort, lustwort, and hogweed, specifically. Also some of my furs."

"Do you know how they got in?"

"BSI claimed it was through an air vent. That seemed to make sense, because I know for a fact my doors were locked."

"And were your doors locked last night?" asked Larry.

Augusta frowned and crossed her arms over her chest. "Of course they were. What do you take me for? I've been double checking them because I wasn't about to let something like this happen again. Didn't realize I should've invested in steel reinforced vent covers, though. I figured if anything, a family of raccoons would move in before I got hit by another duende."

Larry shook his head. "I'm not sure the covers would've helped."

Augusta blinked. "Why not?"

"Because I'm ninety-nine percent certain you're not dealing with a duende at all."

"She isn't?" I said.

Larry shook his head, but he didn't seem as disappointed as I thought he'd be. "No. You said the intruder went after your hogweed the first time. That must've been what set it off. What made it go crazy and bust up the rest of your shop. hogweed is a drug to many wild sprites and spirits. It even has the nickname—"

Augusta gave an exasperated sigh. "Fae catnip. Yes, I know. I went through this with your colleagues the last time. I don't see why it means I wasn't attacked by a duende, though."

"Because according to the lore I've read, duende are sentient beings. They're not affected by hogweed. No creatures capable of rational thought are. Not to mention that while duendes are small, they aren't miniscule. One couldn't have crept through your AC system without disturbing the vents, which nobody seems to have done." He pointed at one of the many vents situated high up on the walls.

I stepped forward into the worst of the carnage. The Smell of licorice was incredibly thick. I felt as if I'd stepped into a candy shop. "So if not a duende, what do you think we're dealing with?"

"If I had to guess," said Larry, "given the plants it went after and the fact that locked doors posed no impediment to it getting in, probably a creature that wields phasing magic. Not a ghost per se. Maybe an ectoplast. I've never seen one myself, but they're sprites that live in our world and the spirit world simultaneously. Sometimes, they don't know which one they're in, so they can act erratically. They could've passed through a locked door as if it were a fine mist. The other option is we might be dealing with a shapeshifter. Those suckers love hogweed, and one of them could've easily gotten through the ductwork where a duende couldn't. Either way, it's pretty exciting. Both of those things are rare as the dickens."

I froze, the icy grip of realization closing over me. "A... *shapeshifter?*"

Larry nodded. "Could be."

A hammer swung, and the ice shattered. "Larry! A shapeshifter! *It was a SHAPESHIFTER!*"

"Hold your horses, kid," said Larry. "I said it *might* be a shapeshifter. It just as easily could—"

I grabbed Larry's duster, word vomit pouring out of me. "No! Listen to me, it all makes sense now—the BSI crates, Tank's crazy behavior, the damn licorice scent I keep smelling everywhere. It's because it was a shapeshifter!"

Larry's eyebrows furrowed. "I'm not sure I'm following."

My heart pounded in my chest as if I'd sprinted a half mile. I had to force myself to breathe. "BSI. They left crates here. They captured whatever it was that broke in. They said it was a duende, but they lied. It was a shapeshifter! Somehow, they coerced or cajoled or threatened it into doing what they wanted."

"Which was what?"

"*Impersonating Tank!* It's the only explanation that makes sense. I kept telling you, Tank wouldn't have gone crazy at the gala for no reason. Turns out he didn't! It was a shapeshifter impersonating Tank in bear form. It explains why there wasn't an ounce of recognition is his eyes when he looked at me. It explains why he attacked me at the country club and the pair of us at the capitol. It explains why neither of our spells affected him, not even your stasis spell that worked on him once before. Because it wasn't him! BSI used the captured shapeshifter to put on an elaborate show to make us think he'd gone crazy!"

Larry gave me another of those caring, empathetic glances. "Lexie, I'd love to believe it wasn't Tank who got shot and blown out of the sky by an attack helicopter, too, but think about this. You're suggesting BSI burned down a country club, nearly had the police commissioner murdered, caused millions in damages to the state capitol, and blew up one of their own helicopters, for what? To fake Tank's death? What purpose would any of that serve?"

When he put it that way... "I... I don't know." Doubts crept in. "Maybe the shapeshifter going *that* crazy wasn't part of the plan. You said it yourself, it's not a sentient creature. Maybe they thought they could control it better than they could. Maybe the plan was to upstage us at the country club and then things got out of hand. I don't think any of the teams we encountered at the capitol were acting, that's for sure."

Larry put a hand on my shoulder. "I'm having a hard time dealing with Tank's loss, too, but you've got to hear yourself. We spoke with Otis over the phone. I know he wants to take us down, to put us out of business, but like this? By putting the lives of hundreds at risk, in a way that threatens their very existence if word ever got out? There has to be another explanation, Lexie."

I shook my head, unwilling to let him convince me. "No. I swear, this is the logical explanation. For Tank's behavior, for BSI's response, for everything. Dawn called me about ten minutes before the attack at the gala started. Tank had gone

missing. That would've been a perfect time for BSI to immobilize him, kidnap him, and swap in the shapeshifter. And the
timing for this break-in works, too. If the shapeshifter didn't die
in the explosion, it could've found its way back to the woods last
night. It would've been super angry, right? What better way to
shed off steam than to return here, smash a bunch of shit up, and
dive into another bunch of fae catnip? I know this sounds crazy,
but if nothing else, trust my sense of Smell. This magical licorice
scent that's all over the place? It was here the last time the
shifter broke in, too. It's not Tank's Smell, and yet I picked it up
at the country club *and* the capitol!"

Larry let his hand drop, and his eyes squinted. He focused
for a moment, and then he nodded. "You're right. It's all over
this place. You're sure you smelled it last night?"

"Dead sure," I said. "Whatever was here was at the club and
the capitol. Even if I'm wrong about Tank, BSI is up to their
eyeballs in this."

Larry nodded. "Okay. I believe you. The question is what
we can do about it."

Larry and I stared at each other in silence. Meanwhile,
Augusta stood there, her face scrunched up. "So... it's not a
duende."

Larry tipped his head at her. "I apologize, Ms. Shade. We're
going to solve this intruder problem for you, guaranteed. But
before we do, we have a friend to save."

31

I STARED THROUGH A PAIR OF BINOCULARS AT A HULKING metal-roofed warehouse in the distance, framed by tall trees in the back and a flat expanse of asphalt in the front. Other than its size it wasn't too impressive. There were a pair of glass doors in the front, leading to what looked like a lobby. Everything else was bare concrete and steel—other than the three letters that hung above the entrance. BSI.

The vehicles parked around the warehouse made up for the building itself, though. A half dozen black Escalades sat in front of the structure, and atop a flat portion of the warehouse, the attack helicopter that had blasted BSI's other helicopter to smithereens stood at attention, its black paint glossy and sparkling in the midday sun. A few vans and a semi truck peeked out from behind the warehouse, but I hadn't seen anyone exit to the back of the lot in the twenty minutes we'd been doing reconnaissance.

I shook my head as I pulled the binoculars down. "I don't get it. *These guys* were worried about us taking their business? The ones who are running their operation out of a giant warehouse instead of a run down shack and have a million dollars worth of transportation equipment parked around it?"

Larry sat in the passenger seat of the Suburban. He grabbed the binoculars and pressed the eyepieces against his peepers. "Hate to break it to you, kid, but that helicopter *alone* is probably worth over a million dollars. And yeah, I'll admit, it doesn't make a lot of sense. Then again, some mom and pop soda company isn't a threat to Coca-Cola, nor a startup auto maker to GM, but you still see giant corporations like that shelling out big bucks to snap up the competition. Better to do it when they're small than to wait until they're big enough to fight back."

"You really think we're going to get that big?" I asked.

"It's immaterial," said Dawn from the back seat. "The point is, you treat all competition the same, regardless of whether you think they're a threat or not. Although given how they've treated us, I'd bet Otis and Jane saw something in us that made them crap their pants."

"Or at least they did in Tank." Larry set the binoculars down in the console.

"I'm not sure it was Tank they saw as the threat," I said. "Sure, he was the one they kidnapped, but probably because they could use their captured shapeshifter to impersonate him. Taking him was a way to get at all of us."

Larry sighed as he looked at me. "Lexie, you need to acknowledge the possibility that Tank isn't in there. That this wasn't a kidnapping."

"We've gone over this," I said. "It all makes sense. The shapeshifter. Its Smell. Heck, the fact that *someone* instructed Olivia to hire us for the gala the morning of the event, *after* BSI captured the shapeshifter and figured out what they had on their hands. BSI wanted us there, and they pulled the strings to make it happen."

"That's not what I mean," he said. "I agree with you. It makes sense. What I want you to be prepared for is the possibility that they didn't *kidnap* Tank."

An icy shock rippled through me as I considered for the first time what Larry was saying. "No. They wouldn't kill him. We live in Texas. The death penalty state. If it ever got out, they'd lose more than their business. They'd lose their lives."

"Then they'd go to extra lengths to make sure it never got out," said Larry. "This is BSI we're talking about, not third-rate criminals who've never seen a dead body before."

I shook my head. "Tank is tough as nails. They couldn't kill him easily, or quietly. Hell, if they'd tried, it would've made the news. A whole block probably would've gotten leveled in the effort."

"I'm just preparing you for the possibility," said Larry.

"What you're doing is being morbid," said Dawn. "What we *should* be preparing for is getting in there." She jabbed a finger at the warehouse.

Larry tossed his hands in the air. "Fine. You want to talk about breaking in? Let's talk about it. That place isn't exactly a fortress, but it's close. Everyone we've seen walk through those doors used the key card reader at the side. Past the glass doors—which are almost certainly made of tempered glass and of which there are two sets—there's a desk. It's not super easy to make out at this distance, but there's a guard stationed there and nothing else, which indicates that to get further into the building you have to get past said guard. Are there other entrances? Probably not, as the one person we've seen park in that back lot came around to enter through the front. Even if there is a back door somewhere, it's almost certain to be locked tight and be tied into a security alarm. This is BSI we're talking about. Security is what they do."

"So?" said Dawn. "All that means is we need to go in through the front. You think we can't take a single guard?"

"I'm not saying we can't, I'm saying we shouldn't," said Larry. "If we blast our way in, how long do you think it's going to be before we have the full force of BSI crashing down on our heads? One we can take, but not two dozen, and we certainly can't do it without alerting everyone and their grandma about our intrusion. To state the obvious, that would be bad. In case you forgot, we're not exactly on the APD's good side at the moment, let alone BSI's."

I grabbed the binoculars and brought them to my eyes. "Maybe we won't need to smash our way in."

"You think we should walk up and press the intercom?" said Larry. "Ask them if they have Tank in their custody? I don't think that's going to work very well."

"Not what I mean." I handed Larry the binoculars again so he could see what I'd just spotted: a trio of BSI employees exiting the front, two men and one woman. The woman was on the shorter side, and one of the guys was pretty slender.

Larry frowned as he pulled the binoculars back down. "You've got to be kidding me."

"What?" I said. "It works in the movies. Like the time Indiana Jones steals the waiter's outfit and throws the Nazi commander out of that blimp, or when Luke and Han dress up like Stormtroopers to break Leia out of jail."

"Yeah, or like when Richard Kimble dressed up like a doctor to investigate the one-armed man in *The Fugitive*," said Larry. "I bet there are even examples that don't involve Harrison Ford.

But those are movies, Lexie. In real life, it's a little harder to beat somebody up, steal their clothes, and trick someone into making you think you belong where you don't."

I watched as the three employees hooked around toward the vans in back. "Harder, but not impossible. Come on. This is our shot."

Dawn didn't give him a chance to poo-poo the idea. "Let's do it. Majority rules. Let's go, Lexie! No time to waste!"

I gunned the engine and pulled out of my spot, racing down the street and barely slowing as I turned onto the service drive that accessed the warehouse parking lot. Blood pounded through my veins, mostly because I'd jumped into a course of action without fully thinking it through. I didn't know what we'd do when we confronted the BSI agents, but gosh darn it, Tank was still alive. I had to believe that, and to save him we needed to ACT! We couldn't let a chance like this slip by, not when every passing second gave BSI another chance to eliminate him and get rid of the evidence.

I pulled into the back of the warehouse lot, pulling alongside the semi-truck so the agents at the van wouldn't notice me. Of course, I couldn't do anything about the roar of the engine, but perhaps if they didn't see us, they'd think me another eighteen wheeler pulling up with gear.

I parked and we all piled out, rushing to the semi's cab. I breathed a sigh of relief as we peeked past the hood. The agents weren't paying us any attention at all, instead firmly focused on moving gear out of a crate they'd wheeled next to the van on a dolly.

"So are we putting a plan together before we rush them or are we just winging this?" hissed Larry.

"Here's the plan," said Dawn. "I'll take the skinny one.

Lexie, you disable the woman. Larry, you get the guy who's been hitting the gym. Knock them out quickly and quietly. Good enough?"

"Something a little more concrete would be nice," said Larry.

"Since when are you the cautious one? Come on. None of them are looking this way!"

Dawn darted around the edge of the truck, her feet dancing over the pavement. Like Larry, I had questions, too, but in my time with the Nyte Parol, I'd learned to be quick on my feet, especially when the adrenaline kicked in. I took off after Dawn, making a beeline for the woman in the group.

I didn't underestimate her just because she was female. She was built a lot like me, with broad shoulders and thick legs, so I knew she wouldn't be easy to beat, especially since she probably had more military training than I did. However, given what I knew about BSI, I almost surely had more magical skill than she did. As long as I didn't let her get to her weapons, I should be fine.

I didn't have much time to think about it. Dawn jumped on the skinny guy, whipping him to the side as she wrapped an arm around his neck. Dawn's intentions might've been to silence him, but he nonetheless got a squawk out before she cut off his source of air. In that fraction of a second, the woman at the crate turned, her hand flying to the holster at her side.

I already had a grip on the magical energies, so I acted quickly. I may not have been a whiz with condensed air or energy bonds and especially not with the sort of time-stopping stasis magic Larry had tried against shapeshifter Tank, but I'd gotten good with wards. As I'd learned from my fight the night before, if you got one of those moving fast enough, it could send you flying. So I slapped a protection ward in front of me and whipped it to the side. The woman grunted as it caught her and sent her flying into the van. She slammed against the metal with a thump and crumpled to the asphalt in a heap, leaving a giant dent in the vehicle behind her.

I was about to pump a fist in the air when Larry cried out in pain. A *whump* of air almost bowled me over. I spun. Past Dawn, who was choking the last bit of consciousness out of the guy she'd attacked, Larry hunched over, clutching his arm. I'm not sure what he'd done to the guy he was in charge of neutralizing, but the blast of air had apparently done its job. The dude lay on his back, tongue half out with his eyelids fluttering.

"Larry. Jesus." I rushed to his side. "What the hell was that? Are you okay?"

"I improvised," he said. "That's what happens when we rush into a fight without a plan. Argh. *Damn it.* I thought I could get close enough for a sleep touch spell, but the bastard was quick. Damn near pulled my arm out of its socket."

Dawn started dragging her charge toward the back of the van. "Can you push through?"

Larry nodded. "I'll be fine. Give me a minute."

"Twenty seconds, tops," said Dawn. "Every moment we spend out in the open puts us at risk. Seriously. Get them into the van!"

Larry grimaced and gave me a doubtful look. I don't think he was doing as well as he let on.

"Dawn and I can move these two," I said of the remaining knocked out employees. "You work on pulling yourself together, Larry. We're going to need you."

32

I HOPPED OUT OF THE VAN AND CLOSED THE DOORS BEHIND me. Dawn smoothed her uniform and checked to make sure the comm unit was snuggly inserted into her ear. "Well?" she asked me. "How do I look?"

"Better than Larry." Unfortunately, the poor guy had gotten the short end of the stick when it came to the uniforms. The black pants hung off him, roughly three sizes too big for his waist. The long-sleeve shirt was just as loose.

"Thanks for the vote of confidence." Larry grimaced as he spoke. He'd refused to take any assistance getting changed, which part of me was thankful for. I wasn't any more eager to see the rest of his decomposing body than he was to show it, but it did concern me that his arm still bothered him. I'd seen him get thrown thirty feet through the air and shrug it off thanks to his magic. In all the time I'd known him, he'd never seemed so feeble.

"Relax," said Dawn. "We're not going to hold up under intense scrutiny anyway. This is about getting through the door without triggering any alarms. Speaking of which—are you sure the people we mugged are going to stay under?"

Larry shrugged. The look on his face suggested he immediately regretted the decision. "I give them an hour. I can't guarantee more."

"If we're in there for more than that, we'll be screwed anyway," I said. "We should shoot for fifteen minutes, tops. Find Tank. Bust him out. That's it."

"Yeah, it sounds so easy when you put it that way," said Larry.

I didn't feel the confidence I projected, but with Larry having lost his, someone had to pick up the slack. I nodded to the others and we headed to the front of the building. I swiped the keycard I'd stolen from my employee through the scanner and sauntered on in.

I'd barely made it though the interior glass door before my fake confidence wavered. A single guard sat behind a metal and glass desk that had roughly half a dozen computer monitors situated upon it. Apart from a lone leafy potted plant that looked like it belonged in a dentist's office, there wasn't anything else in the room. No couches or chairs, no thick rugs, just a single door with another keypad next to it.

The guard's brow furrowed as we walked in. She stood slowly, her body tense. "Ah..."

Dawn ripped a taser from her belt and fired the prongs into the woman's shoulder. She cried out, gurgling and convulsing as she hit the floor with a thud.

"Christ, Dawn!" said Larry. "What the hell are you doing?"

Dawn rushed to the woman, pulling zip ties from her back pocket. "Getting us in the building. You didn't think we'd waltz past her, did you? This may be a bigger operation than ours, but they don't have hundreds of employees. We were seconds away from this woman hitting a panic button."

We hadn't discussed specifics, but I figured we'd have to immobilize the guard, too. Was Larry's brain suffering same as his body and magic? "Is she out?"

Dawn tied the woman's arms behind her back and moved to her legs. "I've got duct tape. I'll hide her under the desk. You guys go ahead. I'll see if I can use the security system to our advantage. Make sure you're on an auxiliary channel." She tapped the comm unit in her ear.

I turned mine on at the suggestion. "Got it. Come on, Larry."

I swiped my card through the scanner at the interior door and pushed through. I'd expected the structure to be what it appeared from the exterior: a warehouse, with high ceilings, exposed supports and ventilation systems, and with useful tools of the trade piled on shelves or sequestered behind fenced pens. Instead, I stepped into an office building. A hallway split in two directions, with offices branching off from the main paths.

Luckily, there wasn't anyone in sight. I gave Larry a nod and started off down one of the halls. I spoke softly into the microphone that I'd clipped to my collar. "Dawn, do you copy?"

I heard rustling in my ear, then Dawn's voice. "Yeah. Just getting this lady stuffed under the desk."

"Do you have eyes on the security system yet?"

"Working on it." She sounded annoyed. "Alright. I've got access to it. Let's see. Where are you guys? Okay. Second screen, bottom right."

"Forget us. Any idea where Tank is?" I froze as I heard a noise. Footsteps? I think they were coming from the floor above.

"Give me a minute," said Dawn. "I just got to this setup. I don't even know how to switch the feeds." My earpiece crackled, the sound of rustling fabric. "Okay. I think I've found something. There are holding cells. A half dozen of them, it looks like."

I ducked as I went under the glass panel in an office door. "Great. Where are they?"

"You think there's a map attached to the security cameras?" said Dawn. "I don't know. They're in a line. But don't get your hopes up. They all appear to be empty."

I reached the end of the hallway and hooked a left into another equally empty one. "That can't be right. Maybe there's another set."

"There could be," said Dawn. "But I'm going off what I'm seeing."

"Are you seeing anyone who could drop in on us and start shooting?" asked Larry.

Dawn growled. "Not at the *moment.*"

I kept creeping. Though the building looked big from the outside, I felt as if I was moving through the halls faster than expected. Maybe the floor plan was split into discrete sections. "Can you at least tell if the cells are on the first floor? Security systems usually have some information about which camera they're on, right?"

"Usually. Let's see. Yeah, first floor, west wing. But like I said, they're empty."

"Any more on the top floors?"

"I *don't know,* Lexie." Her voice grated in my ear.

"What about the basement?" asked Larry.

That made me pause. "What?"

Larry crouched a few steps behind me. He'd paused next to

a set of elevator doors. "There are buttons to go up and down. Stands to reason there's a basement."

I put a finger to my ear. "Dawn? You copy any of that?"

There was silence on the line. It worried me, but eventually she responded. "Yeah... I'm not seeing anything about a basement level. Are you sure, Larry?"

Larry punched the elevator button. The thing dinged and the doors opened right away. He glanced inside. "I'm sure. This thing can go down."

My heart soared. "That's got to be it, then. There's a secret basement. I mean, that's where I'd store a dangerous enemy I'd kidnapped."

"Guys, I don't have eyes on a basement, if there is one," said Dawn. "You're heading into uncharted waters."

"We've got to check it out," I said. "Dawn. Keep an eye on the front. Let us know if there's any movement we should be aware of."

With my heart hammering in my chest, I pushed the B button on the elevator. The doors closed and down we went. Larry didn't say anything, and neither did I. An unmarked basement level without surveillance could either be exactly what we were looking for or our worst nightmare.

The elevator dinged, the doors opened, and I stepped into something out of a sci-fi flick. Cold, sterile white lights illuminated a glass prison, similar to the one the government put Magneto in at the end of that one X-Men movie. The prison was empty except for a single chair, and in that chair sat Tank. He was in human form, wearing the black slacks and T-shirt I'd last seen him in at the gala. Though his body was slumped, his head rested upon his chest, and a piece of duct tape covered his mouth, I was pretty sure I saw the slightest rise and fall of his chest.

"Tank!" I know I should've kept quiet, but the word spurted out of me. I rushed to a door set in the glass and grasped the handle, fully expecting it to be locked, but when I pushed on it, the thing swung inward.

I nodded to Larry. "Come on. Quick!"

"Lexie, I've got a bad feeling about this..."

Larry shouted at me as I ran toward Tank, but he none-theless followed. Maybe he thought an electrical shock would arc out from the lights and zap me as I reached him, but nothing of the sort happened.

I grabbed Tank by the shoulder and shook him, trying to wake him. "Come on, Tank! Wake up! Please tell me you're okay."

My earpiece crackled, and Dawn's voice came through in fragments. "What ... on? Can ... copy?"

Tank's eyelids fluttered. He shifted in his seat before his eyes focused on me. He grunted something that I failed to understand due to the tape over his mouth.

"Lexie, we need to get out of here," said Larry. "This place. There's something about it."

"Working on it." I yanked on the zip ties holding Tank's hands in place behind the back of his chair. "Come on big guy. Help me out. Use your strength."

He mumbled something else I didn't understand, so I brought a hand to the tape over his mouth. "Sorry. This might sting."

He nodded his understanding, and I ripped the tape off in one smooth motion. Tank didn't flinch. His eyes bored into me. "Get out! It's a trap!"

"Of course it's a trap," I said. "Doesn't matter. We'll fight our way out. Come on. Break the ties and let's get out of here!"

"Lexie?" Larry's voice warbled, and he sounded weaker than ever. "Have you tried grabbing ahold of your magic?"

"What?"

"The magical spectrum," said Larry. "Can you feel it?"

I reached out instinctively to grab the energies that floated around me and felt... *nothing.*

That's when I heard the clapping.

33

I SAW A FLURRY OF MOTION AS I LOOKED UP. THERE, ON THE other side of the glass, stood Otis Zachary Pacheco himself. He continued to clap as a half dozen armed BSI agents appeared out of the shadows, but the clapping didn't seem to come from him. Rather, it echoed around me, each clap of his meaty palms a directionless slap.

Tank must've read the confused look on my face. "It's soundproof glass. There are speakers in the ceiling."

The source of the clapping was part of what rocked me on my heels, but it was the lack of magic in the air that shocked me the most. My lips moved, but I couldn't get much of anything out. "What... what happened to...?"

The speakers pumped Otis's voice into the glass prison as he stopped clapping. "Well, well. I guess congratulations are in order. You know, Jane didn't think you'd figure any of it out, but I told her, no. The Nyte Patrol are resourceful little maggots. We shouldn't underestimate them. I'm glad we didn't."

Dawn's voice crackled in my ear again, distorted and unin-

telligible due to static. "... hear me? ... I'm going to ... keep trying
..."

Larry practically growled as he took a step toward the glass
perimeter. "You didn't think we'd figure what out, Otis? That
you're a psychopath? That you unleashed a wild shapeshifter on
downtown Austin and lost control of it when the shock therapy
or the drugs or the hypnosis you used on it failed? That your
heroic defense of the city was actually a kidnapping and
attempted murder that only meets the definition of *attempted*
because you botched it?"

"Murder?" Otis smiled. "If you're speaking about the
shifter, killing it wasn't murder any more than going deer
hunting is murder. It's an animal. A non-human chunk of slime
with as much intelligence as a piece of gum stuck to the bottom
of a shoe. It deserved to die. Just like your friend Tank. And just
like you."

I wanted to correct him that the shifter hadn't died, but
Tank hissed at me, his voice a gruff whisper. "Lexie. We need to
get out of here. Now."

"You think I don't know that?" I whispered back. "What the
hell happened to the magic? Why can't I access it?"

"I don't know," he said. "There's some magical inhibitor in
here. Not magical itself, I don't think. Some piece of techno
wizardry. I haven't been able to turn since they brought me
here."

Larry kept talking. "What the hell are you talking about
Otis? You want to *murder* Tank? And me? Have you lost it? I
know we've taken some of your business lately, but them's the
breaks, kid. Clients come and go. Not like your enterprise is
hurting for funds, in any case."

Otis leaned back and laughed, some of the anger that had

crossed onto his face melting away. "You think this is about business? You think I have a beef with you because we consider your little ghost busting enterprise a *threat?*"

"It's... not?" said Larry. "What is this then? Something personal? Don't tell me this is about that time in San Antonio when you were still single and—"

"*This isn't about San Antonio!*" exploded Otis. "This is about you being freaks of nature! All of you!"

Tank hissed at me again. "Lexie, you need to do something to stop that inhibitor or whatever it is that's blocking the magic. You'll be useless when Otis comes in here to kill us. We have to stop it!"

I reached for my magic again, but I couldn't feel a thing. It was as if the dimension along which magic existed had been snuffed out. I spoke to Tank out of the side of my mouth, trying to make it seem as if I was paying attention to Otis. "Got any ideas?"

"I don't know. Find it. Break it. If we don't we're screwed."

"Short of turning invisible and slinking off, not a lot I can do about that right now, pal. Dawn, are you copying any of this?"

My earpiece crackled again. "Going to ... check map ... I don't know ... going to try."

I don't know if Larry had turned his earpiece off, but if he heard anything Dawn said, he didn't show it. He took another step toward Otis, his hands spread out. "Otis, what are you going on about? Freaks of nature? We work in the same field, pal."

Otis's face twisted in rage. "No. This isn't about *what* we do. It's about *how* we do it. Unlike you, I've had to work my way up, climb every rung of the ladder one step at a time. I didn't cheat, didn't use some filthy magic to solve my problems. I built my business from scratch, using my muscles and wit and guns like any other God-fearing American would've. Then there's your kind. Tapping into some millennia old force like savages, trying to take us back to a feudal system where the one who gets bitten by a vampire or sacrifices the most goats to the underworld gets the power. I don't think so. Not on my watch. I'm not going to let your kind flourish, and I'm sure as hell not going to let you train more of you."

Larry blinked, still in shock. He glanced at me. "This is about *Lexie?*"

I shook my head slightly. I didn't want Otis's attention on me. I had other things to do. Magic-blocking doodads to find and smash to bits. "Not me, Larry," I snarled between clenched teeth. "Make a distraction."

Otis leaned closer to the glass, his lips puckering in disgust. "Hold on a second. Did you... contract zombieism? Dear God. It just keeps getting worse with you, doesn't it? When will you stop? When is enough enough?" He shook his head. "I should've done something about you long ago. The world will be better off when you're no longer a part of it."

Larry kept staring at me, processing what I'd told him as well as Otis's speech. I flicked my eyebrows toward Otis. "Distraction, Larry. Do something."

Larry blinked as he turned back to Otis. He took another couple steps toward the door. "You're still not making sense, Otis. You worked the gala. Your business comes from supernatural folks just like us."

"Most of my business comes from protecting normal, hard-working people from your kind. What business I get from freaks like you I won't miss in the least. Not once I start selling folks the technology to protect themselves from your ilk. Perhaps you've noticed that certain *things* aren't working as they normally do in there?"

I nudged Tank, trying to act casual. "Can you break the glass?"

He shook his head, just as subtly. "I haven't even been able to get out of this chair."

"What if I cut your ties?"

"Wouldn't hurt, but my hands are numb. Can't feel my fingers, and I feel like shit. That technogoober has been blasting me for what? A day?"

Come to think of it, I didn't feel that great myself. Larry didn't look like he did, either. He wobbled as he took yet another step toward the glass. "I don't want to fight you, Otis. Supernaturals. Mundies. We're all the same. We've got the same problems, the same hopes and dreams. There's dark magic, sure, but most of it is a source of good."

"Stop it!" said Otis. "I don't want to hear one more word from your filthy mouth. It's high time for the reign of magic to be over and for technology to take its place. I'll be happy to be the one to see it to its end."

I felt around my belt, trying to find the knife. I knew I had one. "Is the goober in the ceiling? Maybe you can boost me and I can take it out."

"Told you, I don't know where it is," said Tank. "Between getting knocked out and tied to a chair, I haven't had a chance to look around."

I found the knife and slipped it into my hand as I shuffled behind Tank's chair. I'd have to kneel slowly to keep the thugs from noticing. "It's got to be in the basement. I would've felt it otherwise. Larry would've too."

Larry lifted his hands, and he adopted a wide legged stance.

He wobbled again, and the warble in his voice was one of pain and uncertainty. "I don't know what you've done to the magic in here, Otis, but it's not going to stop me. You don't want to fight me. Trust me."

Otis's smile turned evil. "Oh, I'll trust in my technology instead, thanks."

The earpiece crackled again, and I heard Dawn. "... found ... transformer panel ... not sure how it ... going to try and disable ... worth a shot."

"What?" I slipped the knife toward the bonds at Tank's back. "Dawn, can you repeat?"

Larry's arms shook. I felt the strain in him, envisioned the effort he put forth as he reached out with his sixth sense and tried to grasp as much power as he could—but nothing happened. Not even a spark appeared.

Larry sighed and lowered his hands. Otis smiled. "Apparently, I'm not the one with misplaced trust. Gentlemen?"

The thugs around Otis brought up their weapons. One of them stepped toward the door.

And the lights went out.

34

I HADN'T NOTICED THE HUM OF THE OVERHEAD LIGHTS, BUT as they died, plunging us into darkness, they also cast us into silence. The speakers through which Otis spoke cut off with nary a crackle. For a fraction of a second, all I could hear was my own heartbeat, the distant rumble of something that sounded like an engine starting up, and the clack of latch in a lock, maybe Otis and his goons trying the prison door.

Then Tank's bellow drowned it all out. I couldn't see him. Pitch darkness had swallowed us, but I felt his guttural roar slam me in my chest. More than that, I felt his presence. Felt the energy of his being spring to life out of nowhere, same as Larry's did—and same as mine did. It was the first time I'd been cognizant of my own aura. Perhaps all I needed was sensory deprivation to get there.

In addition to Tank's bellow, I felt something else. A rush of air and a gravitational shift. Wood cracked. Fur brushed against me as Tank's rapidly expanding body knocked me to the floor. Normally, it took him half a minute to transform, but from the change in the pitch of his roar, it couldn't have taken him more than a tenth of that. Before I knew what had happened, a giant arm of corded muscle and fur took hold of me, and the roller coaster took off.

I screamed as a burst of acceleration jerked me against the arm that held me. My stomach lurched and I heard another groan. Larry's. His potent smell indicated he was nearby. Tank roared, the pure ferocious bellow of the world's largest Kodiak. I felt the smash as the same time as I heard the tinkle of glass. Shards pelted me, and in that same instant, a wave of shouts joined in. Otis and the rest of his crew grunting and screaming bloody murder.

Another jerk shook me, and I bounced, banging off furry ribs and armpits and with an elbow the size of a waffle iron digging into my gut. A metallic clang rang in my eardrums like a gong.

And then I saw a flicker of light.

Lights blinked to life, casting their cool glow over the splintered chair at the center of the prison, over the sprawled bodies of Otis and his men, over the shattered wall of glass and a mangled metal door, all framed by a concrete rectangle in front of me. By the time I realized I was looking through a doorway, I lurched again and soared. Tank's back legs propelled him through the air. A loud crash sounded above my ear. Pieces of plastic and shredded metal cascaded around me. A dangling cable vibrated like a piano string as we whipped past it, up the elevator shaft. Tank's paws dug into the concrete walls as he pulled and jumped and propelled. I couldn't believe how nimble he was—perhaps the shapeshifter had known better than any of us—but I lost track of the details as darkness swallowed us again.

Not for long. Tank smashed through the first floor door.

Shouts chased us as he sprinted down the hall in an odd gallop that was more human in nature than bear, me under one arm, Larry under the other. His massive weight dug into me, smothering me. I tried to get his attention, but the breath would barely come out.

"Tank!" I gasped. "Tank! Let us go! We can... get out ourselves!"

He didn't slow until we reached the door to the lobby, where he finally lifted his arms and dumped us to the floor. He howled and grunted, and in the distance I heard more shouts. More bangs and clatters of activity.

I pushed myself to my feet, taking deep breaths to replace what Tank had squeezed out. "We've got to get out of here!"

The comm unit crackled in my ear, and I heard Dawn loud and clear for the first time in what seemed like hours. "Guys, can you hear me? Do you copy?"

"Copy Dawn." I grabbed Larry, pulling him off the floor. His face twisted in pain, and he was clutching his arm again. "Christ, are you okay?"

Larry groaned. "No. It's my shoulder. *God damnit.* That escape was not what I needed."

I wrapped an arm around him, taking a portion of his weight. "We'll ice it later. Come on!"

I pushed open the lobby door as Dawn's voice sparked again. "Thank god. Are you safe? Do you have eyes on Jane?"

The distant rumbling turned louder as I pushed into the lobby. What I'd initially thought was the rumble of an emergency generator was clearly something else, a rhythmic thumping that vibrated through my legs. "Not on her, no. It was Otis who came for us. Dawn, are you okay?"

Tank smashed through the door as I dragged Larry toward

the entrance, putting a hole in the wall behind him. He didn't look like he had any intention of turning human anytime soon, though at least when he looked at us there was recognition in his eyes.

The earpiece rattled in my ear as the vibration in the floor increased. "Don't worry about me. Worry about Jane. She's in the chopper!"

"She's in the..." I turned my head toward the glass doors as the thumping vibration reverberated in my chest. Two black landing skids appeared in the air over the parking lot, then a gleaming auto cannon pointed directly at us, and over it, a tinted windshield. In the cockpit sat Jane, earmuff headset on and with aviator sunglasses covering her eyes. I couldn't say with certainty that she was looking right at us, but the maniacal grin that spread across her face as she came into view pretty much said it all.

Larry grunted in pain and shrugged me off. "Get back! I'll hold her off!"

Shouts from Otis and his men sounded close in the hallway as Larry lifted his bum arm, clenching his teeth together in a tight grimace. I felt the air ripple and condense, and I smelled that same timeless mix of fresh sprouting grass and decaying leaves as when Larry cast a stasis spell at shapeshifter Tank at the capitol. The security desk and the computer monitors upon it vibrated, either from the force of the beating helicopter blades or the strength of Larry's gathering spell. Sweat beaded from Larry's forehead, dripping into his tangled beard.

And then his arm fell off.

It slid out of the end of his black long-sleeve shirt and hit the floor with a wet slap, a withered, gangrenous looking thing that didn't bleed at the shoulder joint or even ooze. It looked like the joint had just... rotted away.

Larry's eyes widened as he stared at it. *"Oh shit."* His eyelids fluttered, he wobbled, and like a toddler seeing the sight of his own blood, he crumpled and fell.

I couldn't hear Jane's laugh, but I could see her grin turn into an open mouthed cackle. I could, however, hear the electric whirr of the auto cannon spinning up to speed.

I didn't reach for the magical energies around me. I didn't even think about them. They simply swelled into me as I stepped forward, more of them then I'd ever taken hold. A geyser of magic poured into me at high pressure, similar to how I'd felt when I'd joined bodies with Larry in the spirit realm and taken hold of his powers, but this time it was stronger.

The first crack of gunfire erupted from the auto cannon with a burst of flame. Glass shattered as bullets screamed into the building, but I matched their speed. Time slowed as I summoned a ward of protection four meters in diameter and slammed it in the floor before me like a Roman legionnaire planting his shield before a volley of arrows. Blue energy crackled over the ward as thirty millimeter shells exploded across its face, the mangled shrapnel shredding the walls and ceiling in the front half of the lobby. Tank stared at me in shock, as did Jane from her helicopter.

I ignored both of them as I turned toward the hall. Otis shouted and pushed through the hole made by Tank, assault rifle in hand. He didn't even have a chance to lift it before I hit him with a column of condensed air that sent him and the half dozen goons clustering behind him flying into the hallway. Larry always said magic was like the Force, so I felt the walls, felt the beams holding them up, and I *pulled*. The drywall

cracked and the metal supports underneath groaned. The front
desk lifted off its feet and flew into the gap as the whole thing
collapsed into a twisted pile of concrete, glass, and steel,
blocking the path into the warehouse.

With the perimeter secured, I turned my attention back to
the helicopter. Jane sat there, slack-jawed as the hail of missiles
failed to do anything but shred her building's facade. As she
caught the look of determination on my face, she jerked on the
helicopter's joystick, but she wasn't fast enough.

I doubt anyone could've been against me.

With the same level of effort as a horse shooing a fly, I
finished what Larry started. I gathered a massive ball of energy
in front of me, condensing the air, watching it ripple. I may
never have learned how to cast a stasis spell, but I'd been there
twice while Larry had tried. I keyed in on the scents, the Smell
of fresh cut grass, the earthy aroma of leaves in a forest in fall,
using them to craft the same combination of mystical energies. I
leaned forward, my eyebrows drawing together.

And I threw it.

The bubble shot through the air as the helicopter pulled
back and up, but it barely moved five feet before my spell
enveloped it. I'd only planned on getting the rotors, but I'd
underestimated my abilities. The bubble enveloped the entire
chopper. The thumping blades froze, their momentum invali-
dated. The auto cannon jerked to a stop. Jane sat there, mouth
open and unmoving, as the helicopter fell eight feet through the
air before crashing upon the pavement. It tipped on its side,
resting upon one of the rotors as if it were a kickstand. The
vibration in the air died, and the last of the shrapnel tinkled its
melody of destruction across the battered tile.

Tank sat upon his haunches. Even though he was still in bear form, he gave me a nod. "Gruh."

"Thanks." I knelt next to Larry as the ward winked out of existence. I shook him by the shoulder, the one with the arm still attached. He blinked and his eyes focused on me.

He grimaced, but he didn't cry out in pain when he spoke. "What... what happened?"

In the distance, I heard sirens. I didn't want to deal with the police right now, but I still smiled. "I think I finally figured out how to be a witch."

35

I sat in the front seat of my Suburban as a surprisingly cool breeze whistled past my open window, bringing with it scents of distant rain. The jockeys from Mystic Radio murmured quietly in the background, dissecting the past two days' events as best they could. Around the corner, the lights of police cruisers still flashed red and blue, now lighting up the sky as the sun's rays faded from the horizon. I could've still been out there, but I think I'd earned a break.

Besides, I was *exhausted*.

The lack of sleep the night before had a lot to do with it, as did the toll that using so much magic had taken on my body, but I literally hadn't had a chance to stop and rest in days. Even after stopping Jane and Otis in their tracks, things hadn't slowed. The police had arrived within minutes. There'd been tension and confusion at first what with Tank still being in bear form and him being presumed dead at the bottom of the Colorado River. As soon as they'd caught sight of him, they'd drawn their guns and started shouting for him to get down, but they must've gone through some deescalation training since the last time we'd been involved in a similar event at Tank's ex-wife's Kiara's home.

To his credit, Tank did what he could to keep the situation under control. He transformed back into human form and got on the ground. The police officers weren't gentle enough as they cuffed him for my liking—the poor guy had been kidnapped and held hostage in a basement without anything to eat or drink for a day—but Larry talked me down and keep me from doing anything stupid. Let the system run its course, he said. The police might be hostile and aggressive now, but once the full story came out, he was certain Tank and the rest of us would come out on top.

Certainly, we didn't come out on top right away. Once Tank was dealt with, the police escorted us out of the building into separate cars, though the officers assigned to Larry weren't particularly happy with the straw they'd drawn. Their noses wrinkled as they went to grab him by the arm, and that was before they noticed that his second one lay on the floor.

At least I took solace in the fact that Otis and Jane didn't come out of the incident any better than we did. Officers dragged Otis away in cuffs after breaking into the BSI ware-house through a back door, but Jane was a tougher nut to crack. The poor officers in uniform couldn't figure out how to get into the helicopter's cockpit to drag Jane out, what with the stasis spell in place. I'd found the predicament mildly entertaining, but I'd eventually relented and pulled the spell when I caught Larry's glare from the back of a nearby cruiser.

The back of the cab had been my home for a couple hours as I watched squad car after squad car arrive, as the entire BSI building was emptied of agents and the place swept for clues as to what had transpired. It didn't take long for Frank Connors to arrive. He stopped by my car to ask me a few brief questions, but he didn't linger. He also didn't give me any indication as to what he was feeling. He didn't chew me out or give me any praise, just treated me like any other witness to a crime. I didn't know what to make of that, but I hoped he was simply gathering evidence and not passing judgement.

After a few hours, they finally set me free. Not Connors, but a random patrol officer. They didn't explain anything, simply told me I was free to go. I'd called Dawn first and found out she'd left an hour earlier via cab. Now she was at police headquarters trying to get more information about Tank, but she didn't know what had happened to Larry. I'd checked my Suburban and failed to find him, so I assumed he was still in custody.

Luckily, the officer didn't tell me I *had* to go, so I got as comfortable in my seat and got busy waiting.

I'd almost nodded off when my buzzing phone startled me awake. I pulled it to my ear as the house phone popped onto the caller ID. "Hello?"

"Hey," said Bill. "How's it going?"

"Still waiting on Larry." We'd spoken once earlier. "Hopefully they didn't drag him off to a secure location without telling me."

"To put him in quarantine because of his zombieism?"

"That, or to get rid of a trouble-making wizard when a chance presented itself. I'm still holding out hope. There are a lot of cruisers still on the scene."

"Yeah, I'm sure he's fine," said Bill. "At least I hope he is. We're going to need him."

I blinked, suddenly more awake. "What do you mean? What's going on?"

Bill sounded too light-hearted for another tragedy to have occurred. "Lexie, have you been listening to Mystic Radio at all?"

I glanced at my console. "I've had it on, but turned down low. I haven't been paying attention. Why?"

"Because they've been covering the incident. You think we got a lot of coverage when we took down Benedict? That was a blip on the radar compared to this. They've been talking about us non-stop for the last six hours."

I gulped. "In a good way?"

"Mostly, but what does it matter?" said Bill. "Any publicity is good publicity, and with BSI having basically imploded, that leaves us as Austin's best remaining supernatural consulting and security firm. The story is still coalescing, but I'll give you one guess who BSI's prior clients are calling to beg for help."

"You're saying the phones have been blowing up?"

"I had to hang up on someone just to get a free moment to call you!" said Bill. "It's insane. That's why we need Larry back ASAP. We've got work to do and bills to pay, baby!"

"Sounds like you haven't been paying as much attention to Mystic Radio as you claim," I said. "In case you haven't heard, we don't need Larry anymore. I've got the magic angle covered from now on."

Bill chortled. "Oh, I heard, but you don't understand the magnitude of the offers we're getting. We'll need you both, and more to boot I bet."

I heard footsteps and looked up to see a familiar bedraggled figure in a leather duster approaching the truck. "It's a good problem to have, I guess. I'll call you later, Bill. I've finally got eyes on Larry."

I hung up the phone as Larry pulled open the passenger

door and collapsed into the seat with a sigh. In his remaining arm, he cradled a bundle about the size of a baby, completely wrapped in clean white linens. Was it his *arm?*

"Hey," I said.

He smiled and nodded. "Hey." He looked about as tired as I felt.

I turned the radio all the way off. "How are you doing?"

"Other than still not having one of my arms attached?" He gestured with the bundle. "Could be worse, I guess. Frank told me they wouldn't be pursing charges against me, or you for that matter."

I perked up. "You got a chance to talk to him?"

Larry nodded. "Yeah. We spoke for a long time, actually. Over an hour. He wanted my take on events, and I gave it to him straight. I told him everything. Our involvement in events at the capitol last night. Our trip to Nine Moons. Everything that happened from the moment we pulled into this parking lot, including how we attacked the BSI employees and stole their outfits. There were lots of things he wasn't happy about, including that, but overall he was... willing to listen. He didn't yell. He didn't threaten me, and more importantly, I think he believed me."

"What about Tank? He's not going to prison is he?"

Larry shrugged. "He's still in custody, but I think he'll be cleared of all charges as the investigation proceeds. Frank's stubborn and can be dismissive at times, but he's anything but dumb. He'll follow every breadcrumb and make sure he knows exactly what happened. He'll figure it out. The fact that he already let the two of us go shows he's on the right track, as is the fact that Otis and Jane have already been charged."

My eyebrows rose. "They have?"

"Kidnapping and attempted murder. Yeah. Frank took a call and mentioned it in passing. I don't think it was an accident. If he didn't want me to know, he would've stepped away."

I took a deep breath and let it out slowly. It had been a rough afternoon, but my faith in the justice system was starting to be renewed. "Did you mention Otis's technology? The thing that prevented us from accessing magic in his basement?"

"I had to," said Larry. "The story wouldn't have made sense without it. Frank was curious and said he'd look into it. If it was up to me, I'd probably go find the goober responsible and destroy it, but you can't get rid of technology so easily. Better to regulate it, if nothing else. At least Frank won't try to use it the same way Otis did. He knows supernatural folk are just as much a fabric of society as mundies are."

"And the shifter? Did you guys talk about that?"

"You mean about how we're not sure if BSI ordered it to attack the police commish and terrorize the capitol or if it did all that of its own accord?"

"Something like that."

Larry nodded. "I mentioned it as a loose end that could use more investigation. I also mentioned that the shifter's violent behavior could've been caused by all the hogweed the thing ingested. If so, we probably don't have too much to fear in the short term given it cleaned Augusta out the first time. That said, we wouldn't want to let a creature like that loose in the Austin metro area. Believe it or not, Frank suggested we might be able to catch it for him."

"As some sort of work release?"

Larry smiled. "As a job."

I smiled, too. "Sounds like things are back to normal, then."

"Well..." Larry's smile faded as he looked at the bundle in his arm. "I don't know about that."

I felt like a heel. "Shit. Sorry. I didn't mean it that way."

Larry shook his head. "You don't need to apologize. Really, I'm the one who needs to say I'm sorry."

"We've been through it," I said. "You weren't expecting to come back from the dead, certainly not as a zombie. My actions caused your reaction. It was warranted."

"That's not what I mean," said Larry. "Sure, you made a literal life and death decision for me. I disagreed with it. It's to be expected that we'd be angry and upset with each other over that. But... it's the rest of my behavior that I need to apologize for. When most people get into a fight, they take ten minutes or an hour or a day to cool off and then they approach things with a cool head. I didn't. I shut you and Dawn out. While you struggled to keep the business afloat, trying to battle off Otis and Jane and a werebear shifter and God knows what else, I locked myself in the basement and focused on nothing but myself. I ignored everyone else's problems to try and solve my own." Larry sighed as he looked at his arm. "That turned out great, didn't it?"

I looked at the bundle, too. "Be honest with me. How bad is it?"

Larry frowned. "Pretty bad, but I guess that was obvious when my arm fell off. To be fair, that BSI goon really torqued on it, and then Tank grabbed me in a weird spot as he rushed us out of the basement. Still, the rest of my parts aren't much better. Everything is weak. Everything hurts. The last couple days I've started to have trouble walking. I think my ligaments are decaying. That's not something you think about when watching zombie flicks."

I'd noticed Larry's gait, and I felt a pang in my heart at knowing what he was going through.

My face must've betrayed me, because Larry forced out a small laugh. "Hey. Don't worry about it. It's not like I ever expected to fall in love and get married. Nobody needs to see me naked. If I need a wheelchair or a motorized scooter to get around, then I'll get one. Worst comes to worst and everything literally falls to pieces, we can always get another baby carrier. There are enough of the rest of you to carry me and Bill around at the same time."

I took a deep breath. I didn't want to phrase things the wrong way, but I wanted to be honest in the options I presented him. "Larry... there's always another option. If life, or *unlife,* in its current form is too painful or inconvenient... We can figure out a way to give you what you originally wanted. A journey to the other side of the veil."

Larry's face softened. "Oh, Lexie. No. I accepted death then, but now that I'm back, I can't imagine being ripped away from you and Tank and Dawn again. Not when you're still showing me what true friendship is really like, and especially not when you've only scratched the surface of your magical ability. I mean, seriously, you mollywhopped Otis and Jane and slapped a stasis field over an attack helicopter! Where the hell did that come from?"

I buckled my seatbelt and turned the keys in the ignition. "That was pretty badass, not going to lie. But more importantly, I'm glad you don't want to die for good, because there's someone I want to reintroduce you to."

36

LARRY SAT IN THE MIDDLE OF MIRIAM'S FIRE PIT, surrounded by burning candles and sweet smelling incense. The light of the gibbous moon shone down upon us as Miriam flicked her fingers to and fro, the unfamiliar sounds of ancient Mayan rolling off her tongue. I'd asked Miriam if she wanted my assistance, but she'd politely declined. To be fair, I didn't have any experience curing diseases, but I also wasn't about to sit idly by without learning anything from the process.

I reached out with the full extent of my magical senses, watching, smelling, and listening to every flicker of motion and every word she spoke. Tendrils of power wafted off her, flowing through her tongue and out her fingertips, undulating through the air before wrapping themselves around the magic circle. There, the tendrils surged into the ground before coming back up refreshed and renewed with tinges of green in them, smelling of damp soil and rebirth. The tendrils caressed Larry around the ankles, up his legs, across his torso and over to the arm that we'd bandaged tightly onto his bare skin, the socket matched up with the empty pocket it had left behind when it fell. Larry's eyes remained closed through the process, but I could tell he sensed the magic same as I did. He shook slightly at times, shivering at others, and once or twice he reacted as if he'd been viciously tickled, which made sense given how the magical tendrils caressed him. If I'd had vines or bugs or anything else crawling over me, magical or not, I would've flipped my lid.

Larry took it like a champ though. The rain had held off, but the abnormally cool air remained. Perhaps that was a source of his occasional shivers too, because the poor guy didn't have a lot of fat left on him. His skin was withered and splotchy, sagging off him in weird places. He hadn't wanted to disrobe, but when Miriam insisted we place his arm in the proper spot, he'd swallowed his pride and I'd swallowed my disgust.

The magic continued to flow off Miriam, into the earth and back over Larry. It finally reached his head, fondling his beard and hair like a curious octopus. Larry took a deep breath. As he let the air out, a soft moan escaped his lips. At first I thought it was pain, but when he did it again I realized the moan was tinged with relief. Though I couldn't see well in the light of the moon and the flickering candles, it seemed as if the longer the magic played across his skin, the tighter and smoother it got, and either the shadows from the nearby tree had receded or he'd gained back a little of his normal, pasty color.

Miriam's voice faded to a whisper, and her hands stilled. The magic dissipated from the air, and the glowing green aura that hovered over the fire pit flickered and disappeared.

Miriam sighed as she took a seat in a wicker chair. She looked even more exhausted than I was, and I'd barely slept in forty-eight hours. "Go ahead. You can rise."

Larry shifted, planting a foot in the dirt as he pushed himself up. He wobbled but then steadied himself, and when he rose to full height, he held himself up with vigor. "I feel... better."

"Lexie," said Miriam. "The flashlight."

I'd placed one on the table next to Miriam's chair. I pressed the button on the side and a bright beam cascaded from the tip. I stepped to Larry and shone it on his forearm. There was still a greenish tinge to the flesh, but the black and purple and sickly olive colored portions had disappeared.

"Well, I'll be damned," said Larry.

"Take off the bandage," said Miriam. "Let's see how well the spell took."

I crossed to Larry's side and pulled out the end of the bandage that we'd tucked in on itself. I held my breath as I unwrapped it, but not because of Larry's smell. In fact, the putrid stench that had previously roiled off him had faded to a dull funk, like nothing more than stale body odor.

The wrap came off more abruptly than I'd expected, and I tensed, expecting to hear another thud of flesh against dirt. But nothing happened. The arm held in place.

Larry bent his arm at the elbow, flexing his meager biceps and wiggling his fingers. "I'll be double damned. Miriam, you're a miracle worker."

She stayed in her chair, but her voice regained a little of its strength. "I'm not, though. This isn't a permanent solution. It's not a cure. Nothing is when it comes to the scourge of zombieism, but it'll help. We should be able to control it with regular treatments, targeted enchantments, and of course, with meticulous hygiene."

Larry nodded. "Yeah. That was my fault. I didn't know. From now on, I'll be a smooth shaven, two-a-day bath kind of guy." He grabbed his T-shirt off the table and slipped into it. "So what do we owe you? And I'm not talking about money. Literally, any problem you need help with, we'll be there for you. Just name it."

Miriam smiled. "This one's on the house, Larry. I was worried when young Lexie showed up to help with the wards a couple days back. Not because of her, mind you. She performed splendidly. But I was concerned about you. I'm glad to see you're still in one piece."

"I am now, thanks to you. But seriously. Anything. Anytime."

Miriam snorted. "Of course. But only the first session is free. I'll be sure to charge you handsomely for the rest. After all, as far as I hear it, you'll be rolling in cash soon."

I groaned. "Don't tell me you listen to Mystic Radio, too?"

"We all do, honey." She tilted her head toward the house. "Take care."

Larry and I headed around the side of the home, avoiding plastic flamingos and chipped garden gnomes as we did so. Larry walked smoothly. Confidently. Like the old Larry.

Clearly, Larry's head was in the same place mine was. "I know Miriam did the work, Lexie, but I don't know how to thank you. I never would've thought to call a witch doctor. I would've spent the rest of my days stinking up the house in a wheelchair, swear to God."

I chortled. "Now you know my motivation for getting you fixed up."

We hopped into the Suburban. Larry's door clanged shut as he settled into his seat. "You know, depending on how the future treatments go, I might have to revisit my future plans. Hell, maybe I *will* be able to find that special someone someday. A person to snuggle with, share my life with, or lack thereof.

Probably someone who's undead too. A vampire, perhaps, or maybe a ghoul if I need to compromise."

The engine rumbled as I turned the key in the ignition. "Don't get ahead of yourself, loverboy. I think the pile of work awaiting us isn't going to let either of us have much of a personal life anytime soon."

Larry laughed, which was a sound I sorely needed to hear. I hit the gas, and we drove off into the night.

ABOUT THE AUTHOR

Hi. I'm Alex P. Berg, author of *Nyte Prowler*. Hopefully you've enjoyed Lexie's magical transformation so far, but only time will tell what the future has in store for her. To keep up to date on all Nyte Patrol news and new releases, make sure to sign up for my new release mailing list.

Need more adventures, mysteries, and laughter? Try my Daggers & Steele series, featuring homicide detective Jake Daggers and his clever new partner, Shay Steele. The complete ten book series is now available on Kindle Unlimited. Read it now!

Word of mouth is **critical** to my success. If you enjoyed this novel, please consider leaving a positive review on Amazon. Even if it's only a line or two, it would be a *huge* help. Thanks!

Want to connect? Visit me at www.alexpberg.com or contact me on social media.

For a complete list of my books, please visit: www. alexpberg.com/books/.

www.ingramcontent.com/pod-product-compliance
Lightning Source LLC
Chambersburg PA
CBHW022157260626
47155CB00019B/3063